"I, uh, want you to know, although it goes without saying... I mean, you don't have to worry that I'll, ahem, take advantage of our situation."

"What do you mean?" Melissa turned to face him, soapy water dripping from her hands.

"You're a young attractive woman living in a house with a single man—"

"Oh, that!" Melissa said, astonished. "I never imagined that you and I... Why, you're too ol—"

Old. He raised his dark brows. "I'm too *what?*"

"O-old-fashioned," she stammered. "I mean that in the nicest sense possible. You're a gentleman." She took a deep breath. "Besides, you've made it quite clear you think I'm a loon."

He smiled tightly, still stinging from her assessment. He wanted to tell her that younger women than her had given him the eye. "Loon might be a little harsh."

Dear Reader,

I couldn't wait to go back to Tipperary Springs to write about Melissa, Ally's sister from *Party of Three*. I knew even then that Julio, the Argentinean acrobat, wasn't right for her. But what man could hold her interest and keep her feet on the ground?

Melissa is, let's face it, a bit of a ditz. Her hero had to be strong, unruffled and deeply caring. Gregory juggles a law practice with running a rare-breed pig farm and bringing up Alice Ann. On the surface, Melissa doesn't appear to be the best person to help others. But as it turned out, there was a whole lot more to her than even she knew.

I had so much fun researching the Wessex Saddleback pigs that Gregory raises. I visited a couple of real farms and discovered for myself how delightful and individual these creatures can be. Like Melissa, at one point I was surrounded by a dozen young pigs all nibbling at my boots and pants. I was surprised to learn that when startled, the pigs bark like a dog, just before running away.

I hope you enjoy Melissa and Gregory's story as much as I enjoyed writing it. I love to hear from readers. You can e-mail me at www.joankilby.com or write to me at P.O. Box 234, Point Roberts, WA 98281-0234.

Joan Kilby

NANNY MAKES THREE
Joan Kilby

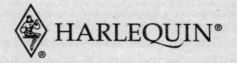

HARLEQUIN®

TORONTO • NEW YORK • LONDON
AMSTERDAM • PARIS • SYDNEY • HAMBURG
STOCKHOLM • ATHENS • TOKYO • MILAN • MADRID
PRAGUE • WARSAW • BUDAPEST • AUCKLAND

ISBN-13: 978-0-373-71437-7
ISBN-10:   0-373-71437-8

NANNY MAKES THREE

Printed in U.S.A.

ABOUT THE AUTHOR

When Joan Kilby isn't working on her next romance novel, she can often be found sipping a latte at a sidewalk café and indulging in her favorite pastime of people watching. Originally from Vancouver, Canada, she now lives in Australia with her husband and three children. She enjoys cooking as a creative outlet and gets some of her best story ideas while watching her Jack Russell terrier chase waves at the beach.

I'd like to thank Fiona Chambers
of Fernleigh Farms, who generously took time out
of her busy work day to show me her
gorgeous Wessex Saddleback pigs
and answer my many questions.

Anthony and Tina Dusty were also extremely
helpful, providing information and anecdotes that
played an important part in writing this story.

CHAPTER ONE

MELISSA CUMMINGS BUZZED down Balderdash Road in her apple-green Volkswagen Beetle, flipping between stations in search of country music. A little Keith Urban would be nice, or Missy Higgins. All she could find were ads and news.

…fine and warm this autumn afternoon in Melbourne…

…woman and two children missing from their Ballarat home…

…two for one at Carpet Emporium…

Dappled light filtered through the towering gum trees that crowded the narrow road. Melissa rounded a bend and shrieked as a figure darted in front of the car. She swerved, barely missing a boy of about eight years old. She had a fleeting glimpse of carrot-red hair and a blue T-shirt before the kid, his small limbs churning, dived into the thick undergrowth.

Melissa brought the car to a skidding halt, her heart racing.

Where had the boy gone? Was he hurt?

In the rearview mirror she saw a toy fire engine lying on its side across the center line.

Slowly she reversed, winding down the window. "Hello, little boy? Are you all right?"

The hot afternoon was heavy with the throb of cicadas and the resinous scent of eucalyptus. A magpie lifted his black-and-white head and sent forth a liquid warble. Melissa gripped the wheel with one hand and worried at a hangnail on the other with her teeth. Had she actually hit the boy? She couldn't remember feeling any impact. But if he wasn't hurt, why hadn't he come out of the bushes? He could be lying in there, unable to move. What if he needed a doctor?

She turned off the engine and climbed out of the car.

Picking up the fire engine, she wobbled into the bush in her high heels. "Helloo," she sang out. "I'm coming."

Dear God, please don't let him be dead.

The dry grass brushed against her bare legs and left tiny seeds caught on the lace hem of her skirt. She forced herself to move steadily through the thick undergrowth. A trickle of perspiration dripped down her back beneath the sleeveless top. She crept to one side of a shrub and pulled back the leafy branches. A small boy, dirty and disheveled, peered up at her, clearly terrified.

"Thank goodness you're alive." Melissa held out his toy. "Are you hurt?"

The child snatched it from her hand and ran, only to stumble on a fallen limb hidden in the grass. He fell with a cry and rolled to one side, clutching his leg. Blood streamed from a gash on his shin.

At the sight of the blood, spots swam in front of Melissa's eyes. She was going to faint. *Deep breath in, deep breath out.* First—stop the bleeding. She couldn't even think until the boy's leg was bandaged.

"Don't worry," she said, as much to reassure herself as him. "I've got a first-aid kit in my car."

"Mum! Where are you?" The boy struggled to his feet, ignoring the blood still running down his leg. His ankle buckled under him.

"Josh!" A petite blond woman popped out from behind a bush a few yards away and pushed through the tall grass. She had a leather purse slung over her shoulder, and in her other hand she carried a plastic grocery bag. Her taupe linen top and khaki capri pants were smudged with dirt, and the scratches on her tanned calves were beaded with blood. When she reached the boy she threw her arms around him.

"Mummy!" A little girl of about six, with strawberry-blond hair, emerged from behind a large brushbox tree and waded through the grass to clutch at her mother's legs. Her bare arm below the sleeve of her pink T-shirt sported a cluster of dark purple bruises, and there was another dark bruise across her cheekbone and eye.

"Did you fall and hurt yourself, too?" Melissa

started to reach out, but the girl shrank back. "There's a petrol station a few kilometers back. I could get some ice for that eye."

"Callie's fine." The woman curled a hand protectively around her daughter's shoulder as she urged the children back the way she'd come. "Josh'll be fine, too." The boy limped on his sprained ankle and the girl struggled to keep up, but neither made a peep.

Melissa frowned, confused by their reluctance to accept help. "His wound could get worse if you leave it," she insisted, picking her way among fallen logs and scrubby weeds after them. "Infection, tetanus, gangrene…you can't be too careful. You really should go to the hospital. I'd be happy to take you."

"Mum?" The boy stopped and leaned on his mother. His voice quavered and his chin wobbled as he fought back tears. "I could use a Band-Aid."

"Oh, Josh, darling." She hugged him tightly. "Of course you can have a Band-Aid." She turned to Melissa with a well-bred graciousness that not even soiled clothing could diminish. "Thank you for your kind offer of first aid, but no hospital, please."

"Okay," Melissa said carefully. What the heck was going on here? "I'm Melissa, by the way. What's your name?"

The woman hesitated, her hazel eyes searching Melissa's face. Finally she said, "I'm Diane. We'll come back out to the road."

At the car, Melissa grasped her large metal first-aid kit by its handles and heaved it out of her trunk. Then she carried it to Josh, who was sitting on a log in the shade of a gum tree.

Diane helped her lower the box to the ground. "This is the biggest first-aid kit I've ever seen."

"I like to be prepared." Melissa knelt before it and handed out gauze, butterfly adhesives, a tensor bandage, antiseptic ointment, scissors and tape. Her family thought she was a hypochondriac, but in her opinion one couldn't do too much when it came to health and safety.

"Are you a nurse, too?" Josh asked. Tears had dried into tracks down his freckled cheeks.

"Me? No way! I'm petrified at the sight of blood." Melissa glanced at Diane. "Are *you* a nurse?"

"I haven't practiced since before Josh was born, but, yes, I'm a registered nurse."

"Thank goodness! You can dress his wound." Melissa's stomach was still churning at the sight of Josh's torn flesh. Bits of grass and dirt were caught in the sticky blood oozing from the deep gash.

"Mummy, I'm hurt, too." Callie whimpered and thrust out her arm. In addition to the bruises, she had a fresh scrape on her elbow. "I want you to nurse *me!*"

"In a minute, darling," Diane said. "As soon as I get Josh patched up."

"I can manage your elbow," Melissa said to Callie, who reluctantly came forward in response to her mother's encouraging nod. "I've got Winnie the Pooh Band-Aids. Do you want Pooh Bear or Tigger?"

Melissa took care of Callie's scrape, then pulled the girl onto her lap while Diane swabbed the debris out of Josh's wound, dabbed on the antiseptic and pulled the gaping edges together with butterfly adhesives. Melissa didn't want to look, but couldn't help admiring the capable, efficient way she worked, covering the cleaned wound and taping a gauze pad into place. Finally Diane wound a tensor bandage around Josh's sprained ankle in a precise herringbone pattern and clamped the end with a metal clip. Brushing the tears from her son's eyes, she said, "You're a brave boy."

Melissa helped Callie to her feet and started repacking the first-aid kit. "If you don't mind me asking, why are you walking way out here in the middle of nowhere?"

Diane gathered up the scraps of wrapping from the bandages, not meeting her gaze. "We…we walked into Tipperary Springs and now we're on our way back to…the farm where we're staying."

"Oh, so you're here on holiday," Melissa said. "My sister, Ally, manages a cottage-rental agency in Tipperary Springs. Maybe you met her—brown hair, colorful cardigans, quirky brooches?" Diane looked baffled and Melissa decided she must have gone to another agency. "You'll love this area. There's hiking, fishing, hot-air ballooning, the mineral springs…."

She trailed off, frowning, as the oddness of their situation sunk in. The town was five kilometers away, a long distance on a road with no footpath. "Did your car break down? Do you want to use my mobile phone?"

"We came by bus." Once again Diane slung her purse over her arm, hefted her bag of groceries, then took a child by each hand. Looking cautiously both ways, she started walking off.

Melissa followed. "Buses don't run along this road."

"I told you, we walked from Tipperary Springs."

The woman looked well-off; it didn't make sense that they'd taken a bus to town and walked from there. And now Josh's ankle was sprained and Callie was drooping like a wilted flower.

"Hop in the car. I'll give you a lift to where you're staying." Diane hesitated and Melissa added, "Your son's leg could start bleeding again. And you know he shouldn't walk on a sprain."

"I don't mind if my leg bleeds," Josh said bravely.

"Oh, sweetheart." Diane squeezed his shoulder. "All right," she said to Melissa. "Thank you."

When they'd loaded the kids in the rear and Diane had taken the passenger seat, Melissa pulled back onto the road. Soon the thick stands of gum trees gave way to small farms nestled among rolling green hills. Diane stared out her window, absently fingering a single strand of cultured pearls.

"Where are you from?" Melissa asked, trying to make conversation.

"Ballarat." Callie piped up from the backseat.

"Shut up, stupid!" Josh elbowed his sister.

"Mummy!" Callie howled.

"Stop, you two," Diane said tensely.

"You haven't come far for your holiday," Melissa observed. Ballarat was barely a half-hour drive away.

"I-It was a spur-of-the-moment idea," Diane replied.

Why would a well-dressed woman with two young children travel a short distance by bus to a small town, then walk out into the country? "This is none of my business, but—"

"Slow down! Please," Diane added, as they passed a single-story cream brick house set back from the road. "Do you know Constance Derwent?" She craned her neck to look back at the property.

"No, I don't," Melissa said, slowing to a crawl. An apple orchard ran along the boundary with the pig farm next door. A sign out front advertised free-range eggs for sale. "Is that her house?"

"Yes, although she wasn't home last time we checked. Stop here, please." Diane pointed, not to Constance's driveway, but to a rutted dirt track belonging to the next farm. "We'll get out here."

Melissa stopped, scanning the cluster of farm buildings on top of the hill. There was a barn, a water tank, a machine shed and an old bluestone cottage. A newer farmhouse on the far side of the yard was reached by a long gravel driveway that wound around a pond shaded by a weeping willow.

Black pigs with pink bands across their shoulders grazed in the sloping green field, some clustered next to small corrugated-iron shelters. Isolated in a small paddock of his own, a boar stood on top of a dirt mound. Melissa suppressed a shudder.

"I think this lane is for tractors," she said. "The driveway is farther along. See, there's the mailbox and a sign, Finch Farm."

"This is the lane I want," Diane insisted as she gathered up the handles of the grocery bag. "Don't bother driving in. We can walk from here."

"Oh, it's no trouble." Ignoring her protests, Melissa turned off the paved road and into the lane, dropping down a gear to climb the hill. Her long feather-and-bead earrings swayed against her bare shoulders as the Volkswagen jolted along the rutted track. "Have they renovated the cottage for holiday makers? If you don't have a hot tub, make sure you go to the mineral baths in Tipperary Springs. You can take it from me, the mud bath is wonderful."

This enthusiastic recommendation was met with silence. Melissa glanced in the rearview mirror and noted Josh and Callie's solemn faces streaked with grime across the foreheads and around the chins, as if they'd already had a mud bath.

Diane was nervously scanning the paddocks and

the farmyard. A utility truck was parked next to the barn, and now that they were closer, a Volvo sedan was visible at the side of the house. "The farmer's back," she muttered.

Melissa parked in front of the cottage of rough-hewn, blue-gray stones. The curtains were tightly closed even though it was broad daylight. Weeds flourished around the foundations and the building had an air of neglect. "You'd think they'd fix the place up better if they're renting it out."

"It's fine," Diane said. "Quick, children, get inside." She climbed from the car, clutching her bag of groceries, as the kids scrambled out of the backseat. Josh led the way, limping, and tugging on his sister's hand as he hurried her toward the cottage.

"I'm sure it looks better on the inside," Melissa said dubiously, getting out of the car.

At the sound of voices inside the barn, Diane quickened her pace to catch up to the children. She put her shoulder to the heavy door, gave a shove and pushed the children inside.

"Thank you *so* much," she said to Melissa from the doorstep, in a rush of polished vowels. "You've been extremely kind."

Melissa put a hand on the door before Diane could close it. The air inside smelled dank and musty. Chilly. "Wait a minute. Who are you? Why are you so nervous?"

"You have to go." Perspiration beaded Diane's top lip and the posh accent sounded strained.

"Please, don't tell anyone we're here. I mean, *no one*."

Melissa's jaw dropped. Before she could recover, Diane shut the door.

"Hey!" a man called. "What are you doing?"

Melissa whirled around to see the farmer striding toward her. He was only about ten yards away, startlingly close. He was tall and tanned, with a lean muscular build and wide shoulders. His black hair gleamed in the sun and his red plaid shirt and rough black work pants accentuated both his size and striking coloring. A black-and-white dog trotted at his heels.

Melissa pressed her palms against the rough wood of the door at her back as she tried to process what was happening. Why would Diane and her children be hiding from this man? Wasn't she a paying guest?

The farmer seemed to be sizing Melissa up with his dark brown eyes, taking her apart and putting her back together. Her hands were damp. She pushed off from the door and hurried forward to prevent him from getting too close to the cottage. She suspected this man wouldn't appreciate being lied to.

And yet she was going to. With luck, he would never find out.

CHAPTER TWO

THE WOMAN HURRYING TOWARD him seemed very young, with rich, cherry-red hair—*impossibly* red hair—that fell past her bare shoulders in gentle waves. What was she doing *here*, anyway, when the house was clearly the main residence?

"Have you come about the ad?" Gregory asked, frowning.

"What ad?" Her deep blue eyes widened and she touched her long, feathery beaded earrings with slender fingers.

"For a nanny." This girl-woman looked nothing like his idea of a nanny. Her black lace top, revealing a hint of cleavage, would be more suitable in a nightclub than a farmyard, and her smooth hands looked as if she'd never done physical work in her life.

"I'm Gregory Finch," he said. "And this is…" He glanced around to see if his daughter had come out of the barn. There she was, poking bits of grass between the wire fence to her favorite pig, a twelve-week-old runt she'd nursed from a bottle. Her long dark hair was tangled and her pink corduroy dress hung down almost to her oversize blue gum boots. Love and worry infused him as he called her away from the pig she persisted in viewing as a pet. "Alice Ann!"

His daughter gave him a sunny smile and pushed her hair out of her periwinkle-blue eyes, the only legacy of her late mother. Skipping over to where he stood, she asked, "What is it, Daddy?"

"I want you to meet…" He glanced at the woman, eyebrows raised.

"Melissa." Her tentative smile warmed generously. "Hi, sweetie. How old are you?"

The child threw out her tiny chest and twinkled up at her. "I'm four. I can ride a two-wheel bike." She pointed to a shiny pink bicycle fitted with training wheels and propped against the barn. White tassels dangled from the handlebars and a vanity license plate picked out her name in red letters.

"What a big girl!" Melissa said, then added to Gregory, "She's adorable. However, I've just accepted a job at a call center. It's not quite what I wanted, but it'll do for now—" She broke off to watch Maxie sniff the ground around the Volkswagen Beetle, then move in a zigzag path toward the cottage. Melissa's hand went to her throat, her gaze riveted on the dog.

Alice Ann tugged on Gregory's pant leg. "What's Maxie doing, Daddy?"

"She must have scented an animal. I hope pos-

sums haven't gotten into the roof of the cottage."
He turned back to Melissa, eyeing her curiously. "If
you didn't come in response to my ad for a nanny,
why did you come up the lane?"

"Well, I—" She broke off again.

Maxie was now running back and forth between
the car and the cottage, whimpering and whining.
She finally stopped in front of the wooden door, ears
back.

"Oh!" Melissa exclaimed.

"Maxie, get away from there!" Gregory called.
"Maxie!"

"The animal must be in there, Daddy. Should we
look? Maybe it's not a possum. Maybe it's a bear."
Alice Ann bounced up and down in her squeaky
gum boots, her eyes shining. "A polar bear with
fluffy white fur and a blue satin collar."

"There are no polar bears in Australia, with or
without satin collars," Gregory told her. "But
maybe we should have a look for signs of possum."

He walked over to the cottage, reached for the
handle and nudged the dog gently aside with his
foot. "Get away, Maxie, so I can open the door."

"Excuse me!" Melissa slipped between him
and the cottage more quickly than he would have
thought possible. Her deep blue eyes met his at
close range and the faint, fresh scent of wildflow-
ers drifted up to him. "I came up the lane to…to buy
free-range eggs. There's no one home next door,
and I wondered if you might have some for sale."

"As it happens, I do," Gregory stated, taking a step backward. "My neighbor forgot to take down her sign before she left on holiday. But I'm looking after her chooks. I have eggs up at the house for her regular customers."

"*Constance* left you the eggs?" Melissa asked. "Constance *Derwent?*"

Gregory nodded, wondering at the peculiar emphasis she placed on the name. Maxie whined and scratched at the door.

"Do you think you could get me some? *Now,* I mean," their visitor said urgently. "I'm late for an appointment."

"Of course. Come up to the house." Gregory dragged Maxie away from the cottage door by her collar. Alice Ann ran over to get her bike, and rode, weaving, across the hard-packed dirt yard.

"I'm one of Constance's most regular customers," Melissa assured him as they started for the house. "Two, three dozen eggs a week. I eat nothing else."

Gregory stopped short. "You eat nothing but eggs?"

"Goodness, no. I mean, when I eat eggs I insist on free-range. Constance's eggs are the best." Nervously, she glanced around to see where the dog was.

"You don't need to be afraid of my dog," he said. "Behind that big bark she's a complete softy."

Melissa gave him a quick smile as she twisted her silver bangles. "Tell that to the polar bears."

"See, Daddy?" Alice Ann said as she nearly crashed into him on her bike. "Melissa thinks there are polar bears in there, too."

Gregory chuckled and shook his head. "You'll see there aren't any bears when I clean out that cottage this week for your new nanny."

Beside him, Melissa breathed in sharply. Out of the corner of his eye, he saw her stumble on the uneven ground in her high-heeled sandals. "Are you all right?"

"Yes, fine." She smiled brightly. "What kind of pigs are these?"

"Wessex Saddlebacks," Gregory said with quiet pride. "A rare breed originally from England. I've got five sows and a boar. This paddock holds the weaners—five months old. The smaller group in the next paddock are growers, about three months old."

"My aunt and uncle kept pigs, the pink kind," Melissa replied. "I used to spend a week at their farm every summer when I was a child."

"Ah, so you have an appreciation for the animal," Gregory said. "They're smarter than some dogs and have loads of personality."

Alice Ann brought her bike to a wobbly halt at the fence and dismounted. "Benny!"

At the sound of her voice, a young pig trotted over, grunting and squealing. Unlike the others, his pink saddle stopped short on one shoulder. His moist pink nose wiggled about, sniffing the air as he lifted his head to peer at the girl from under his floppy ears.

Melissa went to join the child. "Is Benny your pet?"

"Yes," she said happily, and to Gregory's exasperation, fed him a marshmallow from her pocket.

"Pigs aren't pets." He had tried to instill this concept into Alice Ann since Benny was born, five months ago. To no avail. No matter what he said to discourage her, she persisted in treating the runt like a puppy, and consequently he followed her around like one. Worse still, she took advantage of the fact that pigs had a sweet tooth to lure Benny, using all manner of sugary treats.

Alice Ann took no notice of him. Instead, she handed Melissa a marshmallow. "Do you want to feed him?"

"Are you sure this is okay for him to eat?" Melissa asked, glancing doubtfully at the sweet.

"He *loves* them," the four-year-old replied. "Go on."

Melissa stuck her hand through the wire and laid the marshmallow on the ground. Benny gobbled it up and grunted for more. Alice Ann produced a cookie and fed it to him.

Gregory shook his head as his daughter fussed over the pig. Heaven help her—and him—when the weaners were taken to the abattoir in a few days. Gregory had to tell her soon, but he could never seem to find the right moment.

"When's Ruthie going to have her babies?" Alice Ann demanded, running back to her bike. "Will she have to go to the hogs-pital?"

"Pigs don't go into hospital," he replied, suppressing a smile. The heavily pregnant sow was lumbering up the hill with long tufts of grass hanging out of her mouth, on her way to the corner of the paddock where she was making a nest. "She'll give birth right here on the farm."

"Ruthie looks as though she's ready to pop any minute," Melissa said. "When is she due?"

"Early next week," Gregory told her.

"I can't wait to see the babies!" Alice Ann hopped on her bike and wobbled off toward the house. "They'll go wee, wee, wee, all the way home."

Gregory and Melissa followed. He stepped onto the back veranda and held open the screen door to the kitchen. "Excuse the mess."

Newspapers and magazines he never got time to read were stacked on the antique sideboard; bills and work papers were scattered over the red-gum table. The breakfast dishes were still in the sink, the tiled floor needed sweeping and the granite counters needed wiping. Alice Ann's last wardrobe change—a blue T-shirt and yellow cotton skirt—lay on the floor where she'd dropped them. He kept vowing he'd make time to clean up, but there was only him to take care of Alice Ann and the animals, while holding down a full-time job.

"Don't worry," Melissa said, glancing at the exposed beams and the open shelves holding the jars of cereal and dried fruit. "I like it."

"I'll only be a minute." He went into the walk-in pantry and came back with two dozen eggs. Melissa took out a coin purse, then hesitated, chewing on her bottom lip.

"Constance usually charges two dollars a dozen," he said, adding with a dry smile, "Or do you have a line of credit?"

"No, no." Melissa gave him the coins. "Don't bother seeing me out. Goodbye, Alice Ann. Take good care of Benny."

"Bye, Melissa!" His daughter followed as far as the veranda and watched her walk across the yard to her car. Wistfully, she added, "I wish she was going to be my nanny."

Gregory came outside, too. As unsuitable as Melissa was, he felt a slight pang of regret as she climbed into her Volkswagen and beetled off down the rutted lane.

And yet…there was something odd about her visit. If she was one of Constance's regular customers, why did she have to ask if he was selling the eggs? She should have known. On the other hand, why would she lie about something like that?

"HI, EVERYONE." Melissa went around the mahogany table in her parents' dining room, dropping kisses. She'd never thought she'd be living back home, but she'd leased out her own tiny house when she'd taken an extended holiday to travel with her ex-boyfriend, an acrobat with the Cirque du Soleil. She was grateful to be welcomed back into the fold, but there were drawbacks, namely her parents' close scrutiny of her life.

Her mom's blue-and-white kitchen gleamed in the late afternoon sun that was streaming through the louvered blinds. The delicious aroma of roasting lamb permeated the family room. The TV in the corner showed a footy game in progress, the sound muted.

Ally, looking neat and cool in a watermelon-colored sundress, had come for dinner. "Where've you been?"

Melissa hesitated, remembering her promise to Diane. Did that include her family? "I, uh, gave some people a lift, then I stopped to buy free-range eggs," she said, depositing the cartons on the counter.

"Two dozen!" Cheryl exclaimed, elegant as always in a black silk tank and white slacks. "You were with me yesterday when I picked up a dozen at the supermarket. What were you thinking?"

Whoops. She'd forgotten that. "Ally, do you want some?"

Her sister shook her head. "Ben brings home eggs from the restaurant."

Melissa shrugged off the whole egg debacle and sank into an empty chair. Taking a kalamata olive from the dish in the center of the table, she turned to Tony. "How's the olive-oil biz, Dad?"

"Excellent! Now I'm expanding into wine." Tony pushed back his linen shirtsleeves to pour her a glass of Shiraz. "Hear anything from that circus fellow you were so keen on?"

"Honestly, darling!" Cheryl shot him a warning look.

"It's okay, Mother," Melissa assured her, even though it wasn't really. "I'm over Julio. After I followed him to Adelaide and then Perth, I realized that although the Cirque du Soleil was going places, our relationship wasn't. He accused me of not being flexible, but, hey, who can compete with acrobats?"

Ally, who knew better than to be fooled by her flippant tone, eyed her sympathetically. "You're not as footloose as you'd like to think you are."

Melissa lifted a shoulder noncommittally, but Ally had hit the nail on the head. Following Julio from town to town had made her realize how much she missed her home. He, on the other hand, wasn't ready to settle down, and probably never would be. "It was fun for a while, but he wasn't right for me."

"It's a shame, considering you gave up your job at the boutique to go with him," Ally said. "Have you found anything else yet?"

"I've got a job in telemarketing." Melissa fixed an animated expression on her face and said in a singsong voice, "Would *you* like a tropical holiday? Every purchase of $50,000 dollars or more comes with a weekend in Cairns, staying in two-star luxury. Airfaresnotincluded."

Her family responded with worried frowns and anxious biting of lips. For goodness' sake. Any minute they'd break into a rousing chorus of 'How do you solve a problem like Melissa?'"

"It's just for a while," she said defensively. "Eventually I'll find something better."

"Don't wait another *second* to start looking," Ally said. "Let's make a list of possibilities." She pulled a pen and notepad from her purse and in her precise handwriting jotted down a heading.

Melissa sighed. It probably read Jobs Even Melissa Could Do.

"How about waitress?" Ally suggested. "I could ask Ben if they need anyone at Mangos."

"No thanks," Melissa said. "I'd be hopeless at remembering people's orders." She tore off a chunk of crusty bread and dunked it in the bowl of olive oil.

"Farm worker?" Tony suggested.

Melissa shook her head. "You know I'd never get my fingernails dirty. I don't own so much as a pair of blue jeans, much less work boots."

"What about the Mineral Springs Resort?" Cheryl asked. "You could get a job as a masseuse."

"She'd need a diploma in massage therapy for that," Ally objected. "But they did run an ad last week for someone to work behind the counter selling aromatherapy oils and tickets to the mineral baths."

"Now *there's* a career worthy of my enormous intellect." Melissa peeled a microscopic piece of skin off her hangnail.

"You got good grades in school," Cheryl reminded her. "You just never did anything with them."

"I didn't have a clue what I wanted to do. I still don't," she admitted. "I do know that I'm sick of small jobs that lead nowhere and have no higher purpose."

What she didn't add was that she hated always being perceived as an underachiever. Her family loved and supported her, but they didn't expect much. Nobody did, including herself. Maybe seeing the incredible feats performed by Julio and his fellow circus troupers had given her grandiose ideas. Or maybe she'd simply come to a crossroads in her life. But since returning to Tipperary Springs she'd felt stifled and restless for change. She wanted more.

"You must have some idea about what you'd like to do," Tony said.

"I want to do Something Big," Melissa said, opening her arms wide to show them all just how big.

Ally carefully placed her pen on the table and exchanged a glance with their mother. Melissa let her arms fall with a sigh and resumed her examination of her hangnail. It was definitely getting infected.

"You mean, like brain surgery?" Tony asked

cheerfully as he refilled his own glass from the nearly empty bottle of Shiraz. He held the ruby liquid up to the light, squinted at it, then took a sip.

Sweet man. He was such an optimist that if she'd said yes he'd have believed she would go ahead and try it. To him, nothing was impossible, even when he was proved wrong beyond a shadow of a doubt.

She thrust her thumb under Ally's nose. "Do you suppose this is serious?"

"*No.*" Ally waved her away without looking. "*You'd* think a hangnail is terminal."

"It *is* a hangnail," Melissa replied, examining it with renewed alarm.

Ally heaved a long-suffering sigh. "Never mind that. Have you updated your résumé recently? I'll make copies at work for you."

"I'll get it." Melissa went down the hall to her bedroom and came back with a couple sheets of paper. She borrowed Ally's pen and inked in corrections. "I'll have to type it up first."

"Leave it with me," her sister insisted. "It'll take me five minutes and then it will be done."

And done right was the implication.

Melissa felt terrible. Ally managed a busy cottage-rental agency, Mother owned and ran a successful art gallery, Tony—well, no one in his right mind would want his checkered track record. Still, he'd started up half-a-dozen businesses in his life and not all of the failures were his fault. In fact, the olive grove was still going strong. What had Melissa ever done that was noteworthy?

"When I stopped for the eggs, the farmer was looking for a nanny for his four-year-old daughter," she said. At the time she'd dismissed the idea but after this discussion, being a nanny didn't seem so bad.

"What do you know about kids?" Ally said doubtfully.

"I was one once myself." Melissa popped another olive in her mouth. "I could be a nanny. If I wanted to."

The oven timer beeped. "Dinner's ready," Cheryl said. "Melissa, can you help set the table?"

"Sure." She pushed back her chair to get up. Then froze. The footy game had been interrupted by a news bulletin. Diane's face flashed up on the TV screen, flanked by pictures of Josh and Callie. Melissa grabbed the remote and stabbed at the volume.

"...Diane Chalmers and her two young children disappeared yesterday from their home in an exclusive district of Ballarat," the female reporter was saying. "Mrs. Chalmers's car was found abandoned half a mile from the bus station. Judge James Chalmers is appealing to the public for any information leading to the recovery of his wife and children. Foul play has not been ruled out."

A florid-faced man with silver hair told the reporter in a quiet, tightly controlled voice the details of his missing family. Then, his gray eyes intense and glistening, he turned to the camera and begged Diane to come home.

"That poor man," Cheryl said, clucking softly.

"I—" Melissa stopped. Was *he* who Diane was running from? Melissa couldn't say anything. Her family would insist she go to the police. But they hadn't seen Diane's desperation.

"I hope the police find them, poor things," Cheryl added, "and that they haven't come to any harm."

Now Judge Chalmers was saying that his wife had gone through a depression and wasn't emotionally stable. Melissa bit at her hangnail. Had she done the wrong thing in protecting Diane? She'd *seemed* balanced, aside from her anxiety. But was Melissa qualified to judge? What if Diane's children were in danger?

"Maybe his wife wasn't abducted," Melissa suggested. "Maybe she ran away from him."

"Why would she do that?" Tony asked.

"He might have abused her. Or the children," she added, recalling the bruises on Callie's face and arm.

"He's a judge," Cheryl said firmly. "Judges don't do things like that."

"How do you know?" Melissa asked.

"It's against the law."

"Lots of people break the law." Melissa gave Tony a pointed look. "Some of them get away with it."

"You can see how upset he is that they're gone," Ally objected.

"It could be an act."

"Why are you against him?" her sister inquired. "You don't even know the man."

"Why are you defending him?" Melissa countered.

"Girls!" Cheryl interrupted. "Dinner's ready."

The roast lamb their mother put on the table seemed like a feast when Melissa thought about Diane, Josh and Callie in the cold, dark cottage. The farmer obviously didn't know about them, which meant they probably didn't have electricity or heat. Even if they did, Diane wouldn't risk cooking for fear of being detected. God knows what they'd eat—probably tinned beans. Cold beans, at that.

She had to go back, Melissa decided. She couldn't just abandon them without knowing if they were all right. She barely listened to the others chatting about the olive harvest, the new glass artist, whose work Cheryl was displaying in her gallery, and the town's worryingly low water supply.

As soon as they were finished eating, Melissa jumped up. "I hate to eat and run, but I've got to get going."

"You didn't mention you were going out tonight," Cheryl said. "Where to?"

This was exactly why she couldn't stand living at home. Her mother was asking politely, out of curiosity, and Melissa owed her a courteous reply, but wasn't used to accounting for her every action. "I'm going to visit some friends."

Cheryl followed her. "Have you got your key?"

"Yes, Mother." Spying the platter of leftover lamb, Melissa paused. "Can I take some of this meat?"

Cheryl's eyebrows rose under her platinum-blond coif. "I suppose so. Is it for your friends? Can't they cook for themselves?"

"They don't have the use of a kitchen at the moment," Melissa said. Technically speaking, it was probably true. "They're living on cold tinned food."

"Renovating," Ally deduced with a shudder. "I know what that's like. Don't they have a micro-wave?"

"The electricity's out." Melissa rummaged in a drawer for a large freezer bag.

"Let me, darling," Cheryl said, as if, goodness knows, Melissa couldn't manage on her own, and began placing slices of meat inside the bag, one at a time.

Melissa watched impatiently for a moment, then took the bag out of her mother's hands and, grasping the leg of lamb by the frilled bone, shoved the whole thing in. "May I take the potatoes, too?"

"If you like," Cheryl said, astonished.

"Gravy?" Tony offered, holding up the gravy boat.

"Too messy." Melissa zipped up the bag and upended the pan of roast potatoes into another one.

Then she lifted a hand in farewell to her wide-eyed, speechless family. "See you all later. Thanks for doing my résumé, Ally. Say hi to Ben and Danny."

"Will do," Ally murmured.

"Are you sure there's nothing else you want to take?" Tony asked.

"Now that you mention it…" Melissa turned to her mother. "Do you have any blankets I could borrow?"

"For your friends?" Cheryl asked, one eyebrow raised.

"Since the electricity's out they have no heating." There might be blankets stored in the cottage, but she wasn't banking on it.

While Cheryl went down the hall to the linen closet, Melissa slipped behind the kitchen counter and pocketed the salt and pepper.

"Why aren't these people more organized?" Ally asked. "They should have thought of cooking and heating before they started renovating."

"You know how some of Melissa's friends are," Cheryl said, coming back into the room with an armful of folded blankets.

"I should resent that," Melissa said mildly. Just because she was hopelessly impractical didn't mean her friends were.

"How many are there?" Cheryl asked, piling the blankets into her arms. "Who are they?"

"Golly, you people ask a lot of questions!" She staggered to the front door, loaded down with blankets and bags of food.

"Would they like some olive oil?" Tony called after her, holding out a bottle of his premium extra virgin.

"Not this time, but thanks," Melissa said. "'Bye!"

She threw everything into the backseat of the Volkswagen and drove back to the turnoff to Balderdash Road, parking a hundred meters from the farm. She just hoped the dog was inside the house; otherwise, she might have to sacrifice the lamb, and that would be a shame.

Melissa got out of the car with her bundle of blankets and bags of food and walked up the long track to the cottage. The tiny beam of her pocket flashlight wobbled along the shadowed ruts.

The yard was dark except for a pool of light spreading from the bare bulb above the door of the barn. The curtained windows of the house glowed yellow. She tried not to think about Gregory, but his image rushed into her mind—silky black hair, dark eyes watching her....

She reached the cottage and tapped lightly on the door with the end of the flashlight. No response. She turned the handle and pushed hard. The door creaked open.

"Diane?" she called softly into the blackness, "it's me."

CHAPTER THREE

YAWNING, ALICE ANN snuggled deeper beneath her raspberry-pink comforter and hugged her stuffed Piglet closer. Her hair was still damp from her bath and dark brown tendrils curled around her cheeks.

Gregory, sitting on the edge of the bed, reached over to turn out her bedside lamp. "Good night, sweetheart."

"Daddy?" she said sleepily. "Why can't Melissa be my nanny? She smelled pretty. Like flowers."

"Did she?" Gregory asked, pretending he didn't remember, even though he recalled quite clearly the scent of violets and wild roses.

"So can she, Daddy?"

"She's not a nanny, sweetheart. Even if she wanted the job, the question of who looks after you is an important decision. We need to consider qualifications and experience, not just how nice a person is or how she smells. I only want what's best for you. Do you understand?"

"I guess so." She sighed and hugged Piglet closer.

"I'm going to call Mrs. Blundstone tomorrow."

"Not Mrs. Blundstone!" Alice Ann sat up, her arms braced against the bed. "She's a witch. She'll turn me into a cane toad! Then she'll make me blow up like a balloon and 'splode into yucky stuff and fly all over the place and go splat and—"

"Alice Ann. Where do you get these crazy ideas?" Gregory said sternly. "Mrs. Blundstone has many years' experience both as a teacher and as a nanny."

"I hate her!" His daughter flung herself back onto her pillow. "She never smiled at me, not once. And she didn't say hi to Benny."

Gregory smoothed her tangled hair back from her forehead. "I need to talk to you about Benny."

Her scowl faded into a smile that put a dimple in her right cheek. "He's nearly as big as the other weaners now, isn't he, Daddy?"

"Yes, he is. Benny's a fine pig. A *valuable* pig." Gregory paused. This was as difficult for him to say as it would be for his daughter to accept. "You see, sweetheart, the time has come for the weaners to leave our farm."

A tiny frown creased Alice Ann's forehead. "Why? This is their home."

"Not…forever." Gregory cleared his throat.

She straightened up. "But you don't mean Benny."

"Benny, too, I'm afraid."

Alice Ann clutched her Piglet, anxious and

angry. "He'll miss me so much. Why does he have to go away?"

Gregory scratched the back of his head, feeling perspiration form on his scalp. "He's getting big. It's time for him to leave, to go to…a better place."

"How can it be better when he won't have me to play with?" Alice Ann argued. "Where is he going?"

"It's a special place just for pigs," he fibbed, hating himself. "Benny will love it. You want Benny to be happy, don't you?"

"Yes." She thought for a minute. "Is it like the resort Grandma Finch went to on the Gold Coast?"

"Well…" Gregory began, then stalled.

"A pig resort!" Eyes shining, Alice Ann paid no attention to her dad's protest as she danced Piglet across her pink coverlet. "Benny's going to a five-star pig resort."

"Wait a minute—"

"I bet it's beautiful," she declared, rapidly embellishing. "A fancy chef will make his favorite slop. There will be green fields where he can lie in the sun—" with an elaborate sigh she sank blissfully into her pillow "—all day long."

"It sounds mighty fine," Gregory said, smiling despite himself. "The weaners might like it so much they won't want to come home."

"Not Benny." Alice Ann shook her head solemnly. "He's my extra specialest piggy. He'll come back as soon as he can. And if he doesn't, we'll go get him, won't we, Daddy?"

"We'll see."

"We will." She nodded decisively, settling the matter.

Gregory tucked the covers around her. "Time to sleep now."

She yawned. "I liked her dangly earrings, too."

Melissa again. Gregory recalled the way her earrings had cast feathery shadows over the soft skin and fragile bones at the base of her neck. Ridiculous bits of fluff and frivolity, totally out of place on a farm.

"She has a tiny weeny space between her front teeth just like me." Alice Ann bared her teeth to show him the gap.

Gregory smiled. As if he didn't know every freckle and hair on his daughter's precious body. He'd noticed Melissa's teeth, too, though. That kind of perception was unusual for him.

"Mrs. Blundstone will make a wonderful nanny," Gregory said. "She'll bake cookies, play dress up and read you all the storybooks you want."

He stopped, realizing Mrs. Blundstone had said nothing about cookies and playing dress up. When he'd interviewed her, she'd talked about reading readiness and giving Alice Ann a head start on arithmetic. Which was *good* because that's what he wanted in a nanny.

"I'm tired, Daddy," Alice Ann told him, yawning again. "Night-night…"

"Sleep tight…" he replied, falling in with their nighttime ritual.

"See you tomorrow…" Alice Ann's eyes fell shut. In the lamplight her lashes were soft crescents against her rosy skin.

"In the morning light," Gregory finished softly. He touched the back of his finger to her cheek, but his baby was already fast asleep.

MELISSA'S FLASHLIGHT illuminated a small lounge room packed with furniture. There were three couches plus one…two…three…*four* armchairs. There was an outdoor table and a kitchen table, both with chairs piled upside down on top. A narrow walkway next to the wall led around a breakfast bar to the galley kitchen. Cardboard boxes were piled in the far corner of the lounge room. To the right, a doorway presumably led to the bedrooms.

"Diane?" she whispered again, "it's me, Melissa."

A scuffling sound from a back room caught Melissa's attention. Diane peered around the doorway, shielding her eyes from the light with her hand. Melissa turned the flashlight beam on herself. "It's me," she repeated.

Diane whispered to her children to stay back, and came into the room. "What are you doing here?"

Josh and Callie ignored her warning and crept

after her, Callie clutching the hem of her mother's blouse.

"I brought you some food and blankets." Melissa edged between the couches and the wall. She laid the blankets over the back of a couch and set the bags of food on the breakfast bar. From her shoulder bag she produced a large bottle of water she'd had in her car.

"You shouldn't have come." Melissa could tell by the tense expression on Diane's narrow face just how frightened she was. "Someone could have seen you or heard your car."

"I left my car on the road. No one saw me." Melissa began unzipping the bags of food. "Are you hungry? My mother's roast lamb is sensational. I couldn't bring the gravy, but I've got salt and pepper. I didn't even think about plates or cutlery. Is there some in the kitchen? There's roast pumpkin and potatoes—" She broke off, realizing Diane and her children remained silent. "Don't you like lamb?"

"We love lamb." Diane drew in a deep breath and blinked. "Don't we, kids?"

"All we've had today was crackers and cheese," Callie said, "and apples."

Josh eyed the sliced meat and potatoes. "I'm starving."

"Come and eat," Melissa urged, stepping back to make room for them.

Diane went to the kitchen curtains and tugged

them closer until they overlapped. "Someone might see your flashlight." She helped Josh and Callie to a piece of meat and a potato each. "The cottage has been stripped of everything. There are no dishes. No water or electricity."

"How did you get in?" Melissa asked.

"The door was open," Diane said with a shrug. "Yesterday we arrived to stay with Constance next door. When she wasn't home we didn't have any-place else to go. So we waited over there unitl it was dark, then snuck in here."

The explanation only sparked more questions, but food came first. The children ate ravenously, taking bites before they finished chewing the pre-vious mouthful. Diane consumed her food with a refined yet single-minded intensity that was as re-vealing as if she'd gorged herself.

When they finished eating, Diane wiped her hands on a tea towel Melissa had stuffed in the bag with the food, and handed the towel to Josh. She heaved a heartfelt sigh. "*Thank* you. The children will sleep better tonight just having a full stomach."

"You were on the news tonight."

Diane's head came up sharply. "What did they say?"

"That you'd disappeared from home, and the po-lice aren't ruling out foul play."

"What's foul play, Mummy?" Callie asked.

"It's when the ball goes out of bounds," Josh ex-plained. "Now shush."

"Your husband is offering a reward." Melissa watched Diane's face. "He's worried you might be hurt."

"Hurt! That's a good joke," Diane said bitterly. "And he's a good actor. He ought to be, considering how much practice he gets."

"He said he won't rest until he finds you and brings you home," Melissa added.

"Oh, he wants us back, all right. He's short-listed for a seat on the Supreme Court. He'd lose all hope of that if his wife brought charges against him." Now Diane was studying Melissa's face. "I guess you've figured out that I've run away from him."

"We should go home," Josh said suddenly. "Maybe he really does miss us and won't be so angry from now on."

"I'm sorry, Josh, that's not an option." Diane put her arms around her children. "Everything will be all right once we get hold of Constance."

"Apparently she's away," Melissa said. "The farmer didn't say where or for how long. I couldn't ask too many questions. It would have seemed odd, since I more or less told him I was a friend of hers. Was she expecting you?"

"No, but she said I could come anytime and bring the kids. I couldn't reach her before we left. I didn't even consider the possibility of her being away." Diane worried at her bottom lip. "She's retired and lives on her own, so it's not unusual for her to take off for a day or two, but I should have been able to reach her on her mobile phone. I've tried a dozen times and it's never on."

"She could be out of range," Melissa pointed out. "Or even overseas." She paused. "Wouldn't you be more comfortable in a motel?"

"I can't afford it," Diane said. "James froze the bank accounts. I came away with just the money I had in my purse, and most of that went for the groceries I bought today."

"What about your credit cards?"

"Canceled," Diane said. "James talked me into giving up work after we were married, so I was never able to get a credit card in my own name. Anyway, if I went to a motel or used a credit card, the police would be able to track me."

"Do you have any other friends or relatives you can stay with?"

"My family lives on the other side of the country, in Perth. They think James is some sort of god," Diane said disdainfully. "I left him once before. My own mother told me to go home and patch things up because he was a 'good provider.'"

"Well, I'm sure you must have had a solid reason to leave him," Melissa said.

Diane opened her mouth to speak, then thought better of it and turned to Josh. "You kids take the blankets and put them on the bed."

"It's dark in there." Callie pressed herself against her mother's legs, her fearful gaze on the black doorway.

"Josh, have you got your penlight?" Diane asked.

"Come on, Callie." Josh took it from his pocket and gave it to his sister to light the way. Then he gathered up the blankets and the two children shuffled into the other room.

Diane waited until they'd gone. In a low voice, she said, "James...abuses me. I put up with it for years because he threatened to take the kids away from me if I divorced him."

"Surely he couldn't do that," Melissa protested.

"I believe he could," Diane said simply. "He knows everyone in the judicial system, as well as the social-welfare agencies and the police. Everyone either admires him or is afraid of his power and influence. No one would believe *me*."

"What made you decide to leave again?"

Diane twisted the glittering diamond on her left hand. She said, in a hard voice, "This time he hurt Callie."

So it was true. The bruises had been inflicted by Callie's father. Melissa felt sickened by the thought. "How awful," she murmured. "What happened?"

Staring into the darkness, Diane said quietly, "We'd been away on a trip and came home to find newspapers piled up on the porch. I was running around doing so many things beforehand that I'd forgotten to suspend our subscription while we were gone. James was furious. He said it was like advertising to burglars that we weren't home."

"That's an honest mistake," Melissa said. The kind she might make.

"He didn't think so. He…" Shivering, Diane wrapped her arms around herself. "He punched me in the stomach. He'd never hurt me in front of the kids before. Callie shouted at him to stop. He didn't want the neighbors to hear so he grabbed her by the arm and started dragging her to her room. She screamed. He yelled at her to be quiet. She kept on screaming… She screamed and screamed." Diane covered her ears as if to block out the sound. In a voice choked with tears, she said, "James backhanded her across the face and knocked her flying. She was bleeding above her eyebrow."

"Oh, God." Melissa's stomach was churning at the horrible image. Numbly, she groped for a tissue in her purse and gave it to Diane. It seemed a painfully inadequate response.

The woman blew her nose. "I couldn't stay in that house a minute longer. I will *not* let him hurt my kids."

Melissa was silent, recalling the angry purple bruises on Callie's arm and the side of her face. Men who could do that to their own child were beyond her experience, almost beyond her comprehension.

"How did he get away with it for so long?" Melissa finally asked. "Didn't anyone notice? Surely he wouldn't want it known that he, a respected judge, was guilty of wife bashing."

"He's careful not to leave marks," Diane said dryly. "At least until yesterday, when he belted Callie. As for how he gets away with it…" She gave a short humorless laugh. "In public he's charming. He treats me like a queen. Even our closest friends think our marriage is made in heaven. Except for Constance, James has everyone fooled."

They'd been standing in the narrow kitchen while they talked. Now, as if drained by her confidences, Diane sagged against the breakfast bar. The torch threw shadows on her face, emphasizing her fatigue and distress.

Melissa went into the lounge room and took a couple of bentwood chairs off the kitchen table. With a sigh, Diane sank onto one and let her limbs relax.

"How does Constance know the truth?" Melissa asked when she was seated, too. "Did you confide in her?"

"She used to live next door to us in Ballarat. One day she came through the back gate to have coffee with me. The kitchen door was open onto the deck." Diane paused. "Constance saw him hit me. She's the only eyewitness, the only person who could testify on my behalf in court."

Melissa frowned, trying to understand how Diane could have so few resources. "Why didn't you go to the police?"

"Constance wanted me to. But when I told James, he threatened to take the children away from me." Diane smoothed her hands over her pants as if trying to iron out the wrinkles. "He told me exactly who he would call—you've probably read their names in the newspaper—and how he would convince them that I was an unfit mother."

"He was bluffing." Melissa scoffed, but a chill went through her.

"I'd been on medication for depression after Callie was born," Diane said with a self-deprecating lift of her shoulder. "Worded right, it becomes a serious mental illness…even though I was always able to look after my children. When Constance moved away she begged me to come live with her, but I was too afraid he would take my kids."

Whether he could or not, Diane clearly believed it was true. Melissa looked around at the dank cottage hung with cobwebs and smelling of mice droppings. "Why don't you come home with me? I'm staying with my parents, but I'm sure when I explain your situation they'd be happy to have you."

"I couldn't possibly. The more people who know where I am, the greater likelihood that James will find me. He could make trouble for you and your family just because you sheltered me."

Melissa hated to think of the trouble James could make for her father if he delved into Tony's past. Some of Tony's earlier businesses, if not outright illegal, had bent the law. Now that he'd established a thriving and wholly legitimate olive grove, she couldn't have him brought down by a vindictive judge. "Won't he persecute Constance?"

"Probably. She says bring it on. She'll testify against him anytime. I'm desperate enough now to take her up on her offer."

From the other room they heard a volley of sneezes. Diane rolled her eyes. "Josh is allergic to dust."

"That's not good." Restless, Melissa got up and started tidying the food bags. "I wish I could *do* something."

"You've done more than enough and I appreciate it," Diane said. "Don't worry about us. We'll be fine here until Constance comes back."

"Here? You mean, in the cottage?" Melissa asked. "It could be days. Maybe even weeks."

"There's a tap outside the barn for water and we're using the outdoor toilet," Diane told her. "The farmer is away during the day and the farm is so far from the road that no one driving by will notice us if we don't move around too much."

"What about food?" Melissa glanced at the remains of the lamb. "There's enough here for another meal, but after that…"

"Constance has an apple tree in her yard. And we can take some of the eggs. We won't be able to cook them, so we'll just have to learn to swallow quickly."

Melissa shuddered at the thought. This probably wasn't the best time to remind her she could get salmonella poisoning by eating raw eggs. "What about the dog?"

"Josh made friends with her this morning before we went into Tipperary Springs," Diane said. "She was scratching because she wants to get in and play with him."

"Maxie's not your only worry," Melissa told her. "The farmer is planning to clean out this building for a nanny to stay in. Sooner rather than later by the sounds of it."

For the first time the woman appeared to lose heart. Her shoulders sagged and in the dim light her fair complexion turned even paler. "I didn't know. That changes everything. What shall we do?"

Why was she asking *her?* The way Diane's gaze was fixed anxiously on Melissa, she seemed to expect an answer. Josh and Callie had come out of the other room and stood in the doorway waiting, like their mother, for her reply.

Melissa tried not to squirm. The thought of Diane and her children being dependent upon her for their well-being in the immediate future was truly scary. If they knew what kind of ditz she was they wouldn't be asking her for help. But she couldn't leave them to fend for themselves. Until Constance returned, they had no one else.

She couldn't take them to her house or even tell her family about them. Friends were out, too. Diane trusted her only because she'd had to after Melissa had barged in.

Melissa couldn't keep sneaking in here at night. Sooner or later Maxie would catch her outside and bark her fool head off. No, if she was going to bring food and other essentials to Diane and her kids she had to be on the spot. Then she had to find out where Constance was and get her to return home. Meanwhile she had to somehow delay Gregory's cottage cleanup.

She put on a big smile so Diane and her kids wouldn't know how nervous she was. "Don't worry about a thing. I have a plan."

CHAPTER FOUR

MELISSA KNOCKED on the front door of the farm-house early the next morning. She was wearing her lucky skirt, a filmy sky-blue cotton number that fell to midcalf, with a white top. The air was scented by the jasmine entwining the pillars of the veranda, and from the paddocks came the soft grunting of the pigs.

The door swung open. Gregory's black eye-brows arched. "Good morning. Are you out of eggs already?"

He had on a charcoal-gray suit with a crisp white shirt open at the neck. A blue silk tie was slung over his shoulder. Freshly shaved, he smelled faintly of lime and leather.

"I thought you were a farmer," she declared.

"Only part-time. I'm a lawyer." Gregory arranged the tie around his neck and flipped the wide end around the narrow one to draw it through the loop. "Thompson, Thompson and Finch, Main Street, Tipperary Springs."

Melissa heard the thud of small bare feet running

on hardwood before Alice Ann poked her head around her father's leg. "You came back!"

"Hi, Alice Ann." Melissa smiled at her. "How are you?"

"I'm afraid it's not a very good time," Gregory said. "As you can see, I'm getting ready for work. And Alice Ann is going to play school."

"Are you going in your pajamas?" Melissa asked, bending down to tweak the girl's uncombed hair.

Alice Ann giggled and pulled at the top of her Miss Piggy pj's. *"No."*

"Go get dressed, quickly now," Gregory said. Then he turned to Melissa. "What can I do for you?"

"I'd like to apply for the nanny job, after all."

Alice Ann had started to leave, but on hearing this she began to jump up and down. "Yay! Say yes, Daddy!"

Gregory hesitated, glancing at his watch. "I have to be at work in forty-five minutes and I need to drop this one off first, but I guess I could give you a quick interview." He stepped back. "Come in."

Melissa moved past him into the foyer. In the lounge room to her left unfolded laundry was dumped on one of a facing pair of dark leather sofas. The wood coffee table between them was strewn with papers, coffee cups and dirty plates. A toy barn with plastic fences enclosing small herds of horses, cows and sheep took up most of the area rug.

Gregory led her past that room and into the kitchen, where he waved her to a seat at the table. "Would you like coffee? Only instant, I'm afraid."

"Instant's fine."

While the kettle boiled, Melissa helped him clear away the breakfast dishes so they would have a spot to sit. Her heart sank. This man didn't need a nanny; he needed an army of maids.

Alice Ann skipped back into the room. She'd dressed herself in a lilac T-shirt, a mauve skirt that was back to front and dark purple socks. Her uncombed brown hair fell in a tangle below her shoulders. She carried her father's yellow legal pad and pen from the sideboard to the table. Climbing on a chair, she said, "Come on, Daddy. Let's start the interview."

"Just a minute." Over at the counter Gregory made coffee and got out milk and sugar.

"I'll start." Alice Ann picked up the pen and turned to Melissa with an air of great seriousness. "Will you tell me bedtime stories?"

Melissa replied, equally solemnly, "Definitely. I don't always read with accuracy but I have wonderful expression."

Frowning in concentration, Alice Ann painstakingly printed a couple of wobbly capital letters on the legal pad. She looked up. "What do you mean, *ackracy?*"

"*Accuracy* means correctness," Melissa explained. "Sometimes I change the story as I go along to make it more interesting."

"I like the sound of that." The girl drew a big tick on the legal pad next to the letters she'd printed. She turned to her father. "Don't you, Daddy?"

Gregory brought the coffee over and sat opposite Melissa. "I'll be asking the questions from now on," he said. "Go brush your hair, please."

"Oh, but I don't want to miss anything!" Alice Ann stayed where she was.

Melissa raised her eyebrows at this act of insubordination, but Gregory chose to ignore it for the moment, so she shrugged. "Fire away."

"Are you prepared to live on the premises?" he asked.

"That suits me very well," Melissa replied. "At present I'm staying with my parents because my house is rented out. I've been away for some months...on holiday."

"I see. Well, my plan is to clear out the cottage this week and turn it into the nanny's quarters. But the previous owners left a great deal of old furniture stored there," Gregory said. "Until I get to it, the nanny will have to occupy the guest room in the house."

"I'm adaptable," she told him.

Gregory tapped his pen on the legal pad. "I'd like to hear about your experience caring for children. What are your qualifications?"

Ah, now that was her whole problem. She wasn't trained for anything. "I'm really good at playing dress up. I can bake cookies, too. And make things out of play dough."

Good grief, she sounded like a candidate for day care herself. She didn't blame him for that skeptical expression. How would Ally respond to these questions? Her sister would be brisk and efficient. She would radiate competence. Melissa sat up straighter and placed her hands in her lap so she wouldn't fidget. "I did a lot of babysitting when I was younger. Even now I look after friends' kids all the time."

"You wouldn't spend the day playing," Gregory informed her. "The successful candidate will be expected to perform light housekeeping duties such as cooking and cleaning, in addition to teaching school readiness."

"I know my ABC's," Alice Ann declared proudly.

"You're smart!" Melissa said to the little girl. Then she added to Gregory, "Is there to be *no* playtime?"

"I didn't say that. If you're efficient, you should have an hour or so in the afternoon."

"Oh, I'm very efficient," Melissa assured him. "Why, I can…" she racked her brain "…wash dishes and talk on the phone at the same time."

Gregory made a note on his legal pad. Alice Ann did the same, laboriously printing random letters of the alphabet. Melissa craned her neck to see what Gregory was recording about her, but his writing was deeply slanted and close, illegible upside down. His hands were long and strong, the nails clean and well cared for. There was none of the ground-in dirt she used to see in her uncle's hands, although a thin jagged cut ran across the base of one thumb, where he must have sliced it on wire or something similarly farmlike.

"Punctuality is essential," Gregory said, looking up. Melissa straightened and paid attention. "You'd have to take Alice Ann to and from play school every morning, which lasts from nine o'clock until noon."

"Punctuality is my middle name." Melissa made a show of checking her vintage watch, which kept lousy time but looked great with her outfits. Oops. Quickly she dropped her hands back in her lap before he could see that it was off by ten minutes.

"I don't approve of corporal punishment," Gregory added. "Alice Ann never does anything naughty enough to warrant a spanking."

"I would *never* do that. I would..." Melissa tried to remember what her friend Jenny called it when she put Tyler on a stool in the hall. Something to do with time... "Time out. I would give her a time out."

Gregory nodded approvingly and Melissa breathed a sigh of relief. Until he asked, "Can you cook?"

"Can I cook!" Melissa scoffed, bluffing outrageously. "My brother-in-law is the head chef at Mangos. He taught me everything I know." Which amounted to almost nothing although that wasn't Ben's fault.

"Do you have a résumé?" Gregory asked.

"I do!" Melissa was delighted to be able to answer truthfully. She fished in her purse for a couple of folded sheets and handed them across the table. Too late, she realized she'd brought the original, not the revised version Ally had typed up for her.

Gregory perused the marked-up document, his frown growing deeper by the second. He was good-looking for an older man. Okay, *slightly* older. Fine lines crinkled the corners of his eyes, but his hair was thick and lusciously dark. As Melissa watched, a strand broke away and drifted down his forehead.

"Have you had many other applicants?" Melissa asked.

"It's only fair to tell you I'm seriously considering offering the job to Minerva Blundstone, a retired educator with six years' experience as a nanny."

"Oh. She was my teacher in sixth grade." Melissa's heart sank. There was no way she could compete with ol' Blundy. She was very strict.

"Mrs. Blundstone is a witch," Alice Ann said with an exaggerated shudder. "She'll turn me into a mouse, like in that movie. Then a cat will catch and eat me!"

"That's enough nonsense. Go wash your face and do your teeth, then bring me the hairbrush."

"But Daddy—"

"No buts."

With an elaborate sigh, Alice Ann climbed down from the chair and ran into the hall.

"She has a wonderful imagination," Melissa commented.

Gregory's dark brows came together. "Sometimes it can be a problem."

"How so?"

He turned his pen end over end in his long fingers. "The problem is Benny, the runt she's taken a fancy to. This is my first crop of weaners, and Alice Ann has no idea he and the others are going to be butchered. She's forever concocting wildly improbable scenarios about his future. Very soon she's going to be confronted by the reality of farm life."

"I guess it has to happen sometime."

"Her mother passed away a year ago. Even though Benny's only a pig, I hate to burden Alice Ann with another death in her life, another loss. I'm finding it very difficult to break the truth to her."

"I hope you don't want the new nanny to give her the bad news?" Melissa asked, horrified at the thought.

"No," Gregory assured her, "that's my responsibility."

"Poor little girl," Melissa said softly. "I'm sorry about your wife."

"I was never married to Alice Ann's mother," he replied, his jaw tightening. "She—"

"Do my hair, Daddy," his daughter said, running back into the room waving a small pink brush.

Gregory took the brush and started tugging it through her snarled hair. He came to a knot and left the brush stuck there. Tapping Melissa's résumé, he asked, "You've held a variety of jobs, but none remotely connected to child care. Plus there's a big gap in your work history. Were you on holiday for the whole ten months?"

"Come here, honey," Melissa called to Alice Ann. She straightened the girl's skirt, then extricated the brush and gently worked through the tangles, strand by strand. She glanced at Gregory, knowing her explanation wasn't going to sound good. "I was traveling with the Cirque du Soleil."

"You ran away and joined the circus?" he asked skeptically.

"Were there lion tamers?" Alice Ann made claws with her fingers and roared at Melissa.

"No, it's not that kind of circus," she said, laughing. "My former boyfriend is a high-wire artist," she replied. "Our relationship didn't work out so I came back."

"You up and ran off for ten months," Gregory mused. "That suggests a certain lack of stability on your part.

"Or adventurousness." Melissa finished combing out the tangles. She picked a pair of sparkly purple hair clips from the handful Alice Ann had brought and pinned them on either side of her head.

Gregory studied her through narrowed eyes, then dropped his gaze to his notes. Finally he looked up. "Why do you want to be a nanny?"

Melissa opened her mouth, but no brilliant lies came out. Finally she settled on the truth, or as close to the truth as she could get without giving Diane away. "I want to do Something Big."

"Something Big?" His eyebrows lifted, as if her answer surprised him. "Something Big," he repeated thoughtfully, and his expression softened. "You believe looking after children is that important?"

Melissa nodded. She did, actually, although in all honesty she hadn't imagined herself doing it until about twelve hours ago. Gregory seemed impressed, though, so she just smiled and tried to look like a competent, caring mother substitute.

"I'll have to think it over and get back to you." He got up, indicating the interview was over, and held out his hand. "Thank you for coming by."

"Thank *you*." She wasn't expecting the pulse of warmth as their palms clasped, or the jolt when his eyes met hers. "I—I'll need that résumé back, if you don't mind."

Gregory scribbled down her phone number on his legal pad and handed her the sheets. "Your good copy, is it?"

Ignoring his comment, Melissa crouched to say goodbye to Alice Ann and drew the girl into a hug. "If I don't see you again, take care. You're just perfect. Don't let anyone turn you into a mouse, or anything else you're not."

Alice Ann nodded, eyes wide. "I'll watch out for that mean old witch. I'll turn *her* into a bat!"

Melissa rose to her feet and started down the steps of the veranda. "I'll look forward to hearing from you."

Yeah, right, she thought as she walked back to her car. When pigs fly! What a disaster. She gave a last smile and a wave to Gregory and Alice Ann, then put her car in gear and set off. He was probably calling Mrs. Blundstone right now. Soon Alice Ann would be reading at a fourth-grade level. Melissa would wind up selling time-shares in the Simpson Desert over the phone to little old ladies. Diane and her kids would be found and sent back to her abusive husband. And Gregory would believe he'd done the right thing and wonder why he was still lonely.

Melissa drew up with a start. Gregory, lonely? Where had that come from? He was a successful lawyer, a handsome man. He most likely had heaps of friends, not to mention women hanging around. But there was something in his eyes that said he was looking for more. Maybe like her, he didn't even know what that something was. Or *who*. Okay, now she was getting fanciful.

Her mobile phone rang just as she was about to turn out of his driveway onto Balderdash Road. "Hello?"

"The job is yours." Gregory's voice sounded deeper over the phone.

Melissa slammed on the brakes and the car slewed sideways in the gravel. "You mean it?"

"Yes," he replied. "Can you move in tomorrow?"

"I'll move in tonight!"

"You *are* keen." Gregory chuckled. "Okay, then. Come for dinner at six." He paused. "I did mention, didn't I, that I would also expect you to help out with the pigs occasionally?"

"The pigs?" she repeated slowly.

"Yes," Gregory said. "Is that a problem?"

Melissa swallowed. "No, not at all. I love pigs."

CHAPTER FIVE

"YOUR ROOM IS HERE, across the hall from Alice Ann's. Mine is at the end of the corridor, past the bathroom." Gregory stepped back, allowing Melissa to go in first.

"This is lovely." She dropped her purse and overnight bag on the floor and slowly looked around.

White muslin curtains billowed at the open window next to the bed with its burgundy silk coverlet. Alice Ann had picked some dandelions from the yard and wild irises from the pond and placed them in a jar on the dresser.

Gregory followed her in, carrying one suitcase and an open box of books. The room seemed smaller with her in it. The faint scent of her perfume... Her bright hair, her soft laugh, her ultra femininity...it all made him wonder if he'd made a huge mistake. He wouldn't have worried about Mrs. Blundstone keeping him awake at night. But Alice Ann had begged him to hire Melissa, and knowing he was soon going to upset his daughter about Benny, he'd given in.

He set the suitcase on the bed and lowered the box to the floor. A couple of volumes slid off the top. Picking them up, he glanced at the titles. "*Emergency Medicine, Handbook of Alternative Medicine, First Aid for Dummies.* Are you studying for a degree?"

"No, just personal interest." Melissa took the books from him and slotted them into the bookshelf next to the bed.

"Right. Well, I'll let you settle in," he said as he backed out of the room. "Dinner will be ready in a few minutes."

Back in the kitchen, Gregory shifted stacks of papers and coloring books to the already overflowing sideboard. "Lie down, Maxie," he growled as the dog followed him back and forth across the room. Maxie retired to her place beneath an old wooden armchair. "Alice Ann, pick up your toys before someone trips on them."

"Okay, Daddy." She scrambled to her feet and started to gather up her plastic barn and farm animals. "Did Melissa like the flowers?"

"I loved them," Melissa said from the doorway. "Thank you."

Gregory glanced up. "I apologize for the mess."

"That's what I'm here for." She cleared a used coffee cup off the table and took it to the sink. "Where do you keep your plates?"

"I'll show you." Alice Ann dropped her toys back on the floor and ran to a cupboard. "In here. The spoons and stuff are in this drawer. And the glasses are up there."

"Can you help me set the table?" Melissa asked, smiling. The girl nodded vigorously and took handfuls of cutlery from the drawer.

"I'm a very plain cook, I'm afraid. This is left over from yesterday." Gregory drained spaghetti into a bowl and set the casserole dish of Bolognese sauce on the table. A double handful of mixed lettuce leaves constituted a salad. "I'm looking forward to your gourmet cooking."

Melissa touched her dangly earring. "Yes, well, I like to keep it simple, too." She cocked her head toward Alice Ann, who had taken her place at the table. "Kids don't generally like fancy food."

"Alice Ann is an exception to that rule," Gregory said, gesturing for Melissa to be seated. "She eats anything."

The child grinned. "I'm a little piggy. Oink, oink."

"You're skinny for a piggy," Melissa said as she started to scoop noodles into the girl's bowl. "Say when."

"When!" Alice Ann shouted after two big forkfuls.

"She eats anything, just not much of it." Gregory picked a lettuce leaf out of the salad bowl and dropped it on her plate.

Alice Ann ignored it and started twirling spaghetti around her fork. "How old are you, Melissa? Daddy was wondering."

"I was not." All he'd said was that Melissa looked awfully young. "It's not polite to ask," he told his daughter, adding to Melissa, "I beg your pardon."

"I don't mind," she said. "I'm twenty-six."

"Daddy's eleventy-seven," Alice Ann informed her.

"He's aged well." Melissa handed him the bowl of pasta. "You don't look a day over eleventy-five."

"*Thirty*-seven," he corrected. "Alice Ann, tonight before bedtime we'll review your numbers up to one hundred."

Melissa frowned at him with a little shake of her head that set her feathery earrings fluttering. Was she saying he was too hard on his daughter? He tried to do the right thing, but there was nothing like attempting to understand a small girl to make a grown man feel inadequate. "Alice Ann's starting school next year," he explained. "I want her to be as prepared as possible."

"So I guess you read to her a lot," Melissa said, taking a bite of salad.

"Of course." He shifted uncomfortably, recalling his recent battle of wills over Alice Ann's choice of books.

"He won't read *Charlotte's Web*," Alice Ann complained. "It was from Grandma Finch and he took it away."

"You're not quite old enough for that book," Gregory said. Saving a pig was all very well in a children's book, but this was real life, and Gregory didn't want Alice Ann getting any crazy ideas. He turned to Melissa to change the subject. "How do you know Constance?"

She choked on her spaghetti. "Excuse me," she croaked, reaching for her water glass. "My food went down the wrong way."

"Are you all right?" he asked.

"Do you want Daddy to thump you on the back?"

Melissa waved her hands and smiled at them through watery eyes. "I'm fine. Honestly." She took a deep breath. "I hate when that happens. One time my uncle choked on a fish bone and had to go to the hospital to have it removed. It was stuck crosswise in his throat."

"Did the doctor get it out?" Alice Ann asked.

"Well, let me tell you what happened…."

Melissa got only as far as her uncle's ambulance ride before she digressed into anecdotes of her own close acquaintance on a remarkable number of occasions with the Ballarat Hospital emergency room. She described her various medical crises—none of which seemed particularly serious—in loving detail. Her animated expressions alternated between brilliant smiles and round-eyed horror. Alice Ann was enthralled, laughing or squealing in fright by turns.

"Between your books and your experiences,

you have a fair amount of knowledge of medicine," Gregory commented when Melissa paused to take a bite of pasta.

"Yes. Too bad I hate the sight of blood," she admitted, somewhat shamefaced. "My interest is purely theoretical."

"You never know, it could come in handy someday." Gregory glanced at the clock. Dinnertime had drawn out over an hour. "Come on, possum, time to get ready for bed."

"Do you want me to help?" Melissa asked.

"No, that's okay. When I'm home I like to spend time with Alice Ann. You can start as nanny tomorrow."

"Then I'll clean up the kitchen."

All through her bath and brushing her teeth, Alice Ann chattered about Melissa. When Gregory finally got her into bed she was so excited she had difficulty concentrating on the storybook he read to her. Finally she closed her eyes, a lingering smile on her face as she fell asleep.

Gregory sat on her bed a moment longer, just watching her sleep. To think how close he'd come to never knowing her. If Debra had had her way… He shook his head and rose to leave. No one would ever use him like that again.

Melissa had loaded the dishwasher and was running water into the sink to wash the pots. The piles of papers had been removed from the sideboard and the toys cleared off the floor.

"I didn't expect you to start work until tomorrow, but thank you." Gregory picked up the pot with the remains of the spaghetti and sauce and went to scrape it into the garbage.

"Don't throw that away!" Melissa exclaimed.

Gregory paused, eyebrows raised. "It's barely enough for one person."

"I'll have it for lunch tomorrow."

"You don't have to eat scraps."

Melissa tugged on her earring and eyed the leftovers as if they were all that stood between her and starvation.

"I know there isn't much food in the fridge," he said defensively. "I haven't had time to shop, and anyway, I thought you'd like to shop for groceries tomorrow after you drop Alice Ann off at play school. You know what you'll need for meals."

"Still, I hate to waste food."

"Okay," Gregory said with a shrug.

Melissa put the pots in the hot soapy water to soak. Gregory searched a bottom drawer for a plastic container. For a few minutes they worked in quiet domesticity. His glance returned to her time and again. She wore a frilly gingham apron that looked brand-new and which contrasted prettily with her sleek skirt and top. He found himself noticing how her hip curved outward from the green-and-white-checked bow at her waist.

Gregory cleared his throat. "I, uh, want you to know, although it goes without saying... I mean, you don't have to worry that I'll, ahem, take advantage of our situation."

"What do you mean?" Melissa turned to face him, soapy water dripping from her hands.

"You're a young, attractive woman living in a house with a single man—"

"Oh, that!" She seemed astonished. "I never imagined that you and I... Why, you're too ol—"

Old. He raised his dark brows. "I'm too *what?*"

"Ol-old-fashioned," she stammered. "I mean that in the nicest sense possible. You're a gentleman." She took a deep breath. "Besides, you've made it quite clear you think I'm a loon."

He smiled tightly, still stinging from her assessment. He wanted to tell her that younger women than her had given him the eye. "Loon might be a little harsh."

"I promise you, Mr. Finch—"

"Gregory."

"*Gregory.* Even if I'm not as sensible and disciplined as Mrs. Blundstone, I'll take very good care of Alice Ann."

She was doing it again, deflecting his comment. Oh, well, he'd obviously embarrassed her. "I know you will. That's why I hired you."

"And I'll do my best with the housekeeping," she hurriedly added. "I mean, I *know* I'll do a great job at cooking and cleaning and...and helping with the pigs."

"I have every confidence in you," he assured her. "If Alice Ann is happy, I'm happy. In fact, I consider you a godsend. You could be the saving of me and Alice Ann."

"Oh, don't say that!" Melissa cried, clearly horrified. "I've never saved anyone in my life." She turned back to the sink and plunged her arms into the sudsy water, clanging pots together, muttering under her breath, "I'm just trying to do my best. No one can expect anything more. If I screw up it won't be *my* fault people trusted me."

Okay, maybe there *was* a loony element in her makeup, but it was rather endearing. "I'll leave you to it," he said, picking up his briefcase from the sideboard. "I've got paperwork to do."

MELISSA GAVE TWO QUICK knocks followed by two slow ones, then slipped through the door into the cottage. She was unloading her booty onto the kitchen counter when Diane and her kids emerged from the bedroom. Although it was nearly midnight, they were fully dressed. Callie wore what must have been one of Diane's cardigans; the hem brushed her calves and the sleeves bunched all the way up her arms. Josh wore a hooded jacket and had both hands thrust in the front pocket. Diane shivered in short sleeves.

When Melissa took off her fleece jacket and handed it to her, she immediately began to protest. Melissa cut her off even though she was left wearing only her pajamas. "Keep it. I've got a cardigan in the car."

"I wish I'd brought more practical clothes," Diane said. "I had no idea I'd be sleeping in a cottage and not in Constance's guest room."

"Do you have anything for us to eat?" Callie asked.

"Shh, Callie, that's not polite," Josh said, looking every bit as hopeful as his sister.

"There's only a bit of spaghetti Bolognese, but I heated it up in the microwave," she told them. "There's also half a loaf of bread, some peanut butter and Vegemite and a packet of cookies."

"Thank you," Diane said, handing forks to Josh and Callie. "It's strange how you can get hungry even when you do nothing all day." She took a bite and left the rest to the children, then proceeded to make sandwiches by the dull beam of a flashlight. "I was wondering if we would see you again."

"You'll see me every day from now on," Melissa told her. "I got a job here as Alice Ann's nanny."

Diane glanced up from the sandwich. "You didn't do this because of us, did you?"

Melissa shrugged. "Alice Ann's cute as a button so it's no hardship."

"What's the farmer like?"

"Pretty hot for an older man," Melissa said. "But too serious." The truth was, when he looked at her with those penetrating dark eyes she felt as if he knew exactly what she was thinking. And that was unnerving, given that she was hiding a trio of runaways on his property. "He's not my type."

"I didn't ask if you were going to marry him," Diane said, laughing. Then she reached over to squeeze Melissa's hand. "You've gone to so much trouble. I can't tell you how much I appreciate it…" She blinked suddenly. "I'm not used to such kindness. We have a gardener and a cleaning woman. James has numerous law colleagues, but because of him I don't have many friends." She paused. "I'll repay you someday, somehow. In the meantime we're eating the farmer's food. Isn't he going to notice?"

"Nah," Melissa said with more conviction than she felt. "He's wrapped up in his work and his daughter. I'll buy extra groceries out of my own money. You can repay me whenever you're able." She rubbed her arms to warm them. "The bad news is, we're going to be eating my cooking from now on, and frankly, that's not something to look forward to."

"I could help you make up a grocery list and plan some meals," Diane said. "I'm a pretty good cook— we were constantly entertaining lawyers and judges."

"The farmer's a lawyer," Melissa said. "Maybe you know him. Gregory Finch."

The knife Diane was holding clattered onto the counter. Her eyes grew huge in the dim light. "Gregory was at our house for a dinner party last summer. He used to be a student of James's."

GREGORY WOKE ABRUPTLY. His room was dark and the house was silent. A glance at the clock told him it was ten minutes past midnight. Normally he slept soundly, but tonight he'd had a hard time falling asleep and his slumber had been fitful, his dreams full of feathers.

He was about to turn over and go back to sleep when he heard the creak of the kitchen door closing. Sitting up in bed, he strained to listen. Was there a prowler?

He threw back the covers and got out of bed. Dressed only in his black knit boxers, he grabbed the cricket bat he kept next to the door and went into the hall. A light shone in the kitchen.

He moved stealthily down the hall in his bare feet, bat held aloft. Alice Ann's door was ajar, and a glance reassured him that she was fast asleep. Melissa's door, next to Alice Ann's, was shut. He came around the corner into the kitchen doorway and let the cricket bat drop to his side.

"What on earth are you doing?"

Melissa whirled away from the sink, saw him and shrieked. Clapping a hand over her mouth, she put her other hand on her heart. "Don't sneak up on me like that!"

Gregory sniffed the air. "What's that smell?"

"Spaghetti Bolognese. I—I..." She ducked her head with a sheepish smile. "I got hungry. So I heated up the leftovers."

He scratched the back of his head, perplexed.

How did the woman stay so thin if she ate in the middle of the night? He hoped she wasn't bulimic. "I thought I heard the door."

"Oh, that. I went outside. To my car. To get my sweater." She tugged her cropped green cardigan closer around her middle. Beneath it she wore low-slung, cotton drawstring pajama bottoms and a sleeveless top. Between them, pale flesh curved from her hip to her lower ribs.

Her gaze drifted from his eyes to his bare chest to his clinging boxers. A look of surprise came over her face.

Oh, boy. Gregory positioned the cricket bat in front of his wicket and behaved like the gentleman she believed him to be. "Pardon me for disturbing you," he said stiffly. "I'll say good-night."

CHAPTER SIX

MELISSA STRUGGLED into consciousness, helped along by the aroma of bacon and coffee. She stretched her arms over her head and twisted luxuriously in bed. Tony must be cooking this morning. Mother never made bacon.

Slowly she opened her eyes and focused on the unfamiliar surroundings. Oh, hell. It wasn't a dream. She was living at the farmhouse, working as a nanny, a housekeeper and a part-time saver of lives. Overnight she'd gone from being a hopeless ditz to the protector of a runaway mum and her children, plus a surrogate wife and mother to a widower and his daughter. Life had been so much easier when no one expected anything of her.

Melissa sank back onto the pillow and let her eyes drift shut again. A second later she sat bolt upright. *She* was supposed to be making breakfast!

Hurriedly she dressed in the "farm clothes" she'd bought yesterday—blue jeans, a paisley shirt and a fringed vest—and went out to the kitchen. Gregory turned away from the stove, wearing her green gingham apron over his white business shirt and charcoal pants. Somehow the apron empha- sized his size and masculinity instead of detract- ing from it.

"Have a seat," he said. "Breakfast is ready."

"Hi, Melissa," Alice Ann mumbled through a mouthful of scrambled egg.

"Hi, honey." She tucked a strand of hair behind the child's ear as she passed the table. "Sorry, I slept in," she said to Gregory, and went to the sink for a drink of water. She stared at the empty spa- ghetti container she'd left there with *three* forks sticking out of it.

"What is it?" Gregory asked, glancing over.

"Nothing!" She tipped over the container, scat- tering the forks, and moved away. "I'll make cof- fee. Yessir, there's nothing like a cup of java in the morning."

He hovered, spatula in hand. "Do you know how to use an espresso machine? My brother gave it to me last year for Christmas, but I never have time to figure it out."

"I'll give it a go." Melissa squinted at the Italian instructions on the back of the machine. If only she hadn't wasted her time studying German at school. Giving up on the instructions, she studied the gad- get itself. The coffee must go in that circular tray thingy, she decided, which slotted into the stainless steel holder.

She added coffee grounds, filled the reservoir

and pressed a button. "So you're a lawyer. What kind?"

Gregory cracked two more eggs into the frying pan next to the bacon. "Family law, mostly."

"How interesting." With the espresso machine emitting gurgling sounds, Melissa gave him her full attention. Diane was going to need a lawyer. So what if James knew Gregory? He probably knew every lawyer in the state. "I suppose you do a lot of custody cases."

"It's my bread and butter, so to speak." He took out a couple of slices of wholemeal bread. "Do you want toast?"

"Yes, thank you. So if you had a situation where a woman was being physically abused by her husband, would she be likely to get custody of the children in a divorce?"

"Nine times out of ten the woman gets custody whether she deserves it or not," Gregory retorted.

Melissa cocked her head at the bitterness in his voice. "Why wouldn't she deserve it?"

"Look out," Gregory said, pointing at the espresso machine. A thin stream of strong dark coffee was splashing onto the heated tray, giving off an acrid smell. Melissa hastily jammed a glass beneath the spigot to catch the trickle of liquid.

"Why are you asking? Do you know someone going through a divorce?"

"A friend," Melissa answered noncommittally. And then she heard a cracking sound. The glass filling with scalding coffee broke and clattered to the floor. Thick dark brew splattered across the tiles.

Gregory leaped forward to turn off the gurgling espresso machine. "That was a water glass you put under there, not meant for latte."

"Sorry." She crouched to pick up the broken shards. "I'll try again."

"I think we've had enough excitement for one morning. Instant will be fine, after all." He paused, then suggested, "If your friend wants to, she can give me a call at the office." The toast popped and Gregory put it on a plate. "Peanut butter or jam?"

"Peanut butter," Melissa stated, then remembered she'd left the jar at the cottage. "On second thought, I'll have jam, please." She tossed the pieces of glass in the rubbish bin and wiped up the spilled coffee.

"That's odd," he murmured, poking his head into the pantry. "I could have sworn there was a whole jar of peanut butter in here yesterday."

Melissa's heart sped up. "Jam's fine, honestly."

"And another loaf of bread and a packet of chocolate cookies. Alice Ann, have you been feeding that pig people food again?"

Alice Ann's wide-eyed gaze met Melissa's. Melissa bit her lip to quell a smile, wondering which of them was more guilty. "These bacon and eggs look done," she called to Gregory. "Come and eat. I'll worry about the groceries."

He emerged from the pantry and sat at the table

while Melissa dished up breakfast, making a mental note that he liked his eggs easy over.

"What about you?" Gregory asked.

"I'll eat later," she said. "What time does Alice Ann have to be at play school?"

"Nine o'clock. You pick her up at noon. I've let her teacher know you're coming."

"My teacher's name is Judy," the child said. "We've got a bunny rabbit there." She chatted about play school until Gregory told her to eat up or she'd be late. Then he left to finish getting ready for work.

Melissa watched Alice Ann brush her teeth, to make sure she was doing it properly, and was combing out the girl's hair when Gregory came in to kiss his daughter goodbye. "See you tonight, possum," he said, caressing her cheek.

He lifted his gaze to Melissa just at that moment, and she had the strangest sensation she could feel his hand on *her* cheek. Their eyes connected, and both of them quickly glanced away.

He was out the door before Melissa noticed his briefcase lying on the sideboard, where he'd forgotten it. She ran out with it and met him coming back around the side of the house. They bumped into each other, sending Melissa bouncing backward. The briefcase flew out of her hand and burst open when it hit the ground. Papers lifted in the breeze and fluttered away.

"Sorry!" She ran around in circles after the

flying papers, snatching them out of the air. "I didn't expect to meet you like that."

Gregory crouched in the gravel, methodically retrieving files and papers nearest him and placing them back in his briefcase. His polished shoes acquired a coating of dust stirred up by Melissa's efforts. "I forgot to ask you to collect the eggs."

"I was just thinking about the eggs!" She thrust a loose stack of papers into his briefcase. "Maybe we have a telepathic connection."

"If that were true I would have known you were going to barrel around the corner just now, and I'd have stepped aside."

Gregory took the papers and tapped the edges on the top of the briefcase to straighten them. He arranged the file folders neatly inside, then snapped the lid shut. Standing, he adjusted his tie and smoothed his hair back.

"Wait. You have dust on your pants." Melissa brushed at the gray cloth. Beneath the fine wool blend his thigh was warm, solid and surprisingly muscular. Abruptly, she stopped brushing. "I should let you go."

One eyebrow arched. "To torment another day?"

"If that's the way you put it…" She flicked back her hair, brushed down her skirt and spun on her heel. She couldn't resist glancing back. "See you tonight."

His mouth turned up, creating a dimple in his right cheek. "With luck I'll see you first."

"THIS CAR IS LIKE an apple," Alice Ann said as she climbed into the backseat. "A Granny Smith apple."

Melissa held the seat forward. "Don't forget you've got your cardigan in your backpack in case the weather changes."

"I won't," the girl said, holding up her arms so she could be buckled in.

Melissa straightened, glancing past the cottage with its drawn curtains to Constance Derwent's house, just visible through the apple orchard that bordered her property. Still no sign of activity.

The trip into Tipperary Springs took only ten minutes, and soon she and Alice Ann pulled up in front of the play school. Melissa went inside and introduced herself to Judy, a petite woman in jeans and a muslin shirt.

"Hi, Alice Ann," her teacher said, bending down to give the girl a big smile. "Hang up your backpack, then you can draw or do a puzzle until the rest of the kids are here."

"Does she have any special friends?" Melissa asked, as she and Judy watched her approach a low table, where a blond girl sat drawing with crayons on butcher paper.

"She and Amy are pretty good mates," Judy said, nodding at the pair.

"I can draw a pig," Alice Ann announced as she sat down next to Amy. "My nanny showed me."

Melissa smiled. *My nanny.* What a sweetheart.

"Pigs aren't black," Amy said, glancing sideways as Alice Ann began to draw.

"*My* pigs are." Alice Ann looked over to Melissa as if she was the font of all knowledge. "Aren't they, Melissa?"

"They certainly are." She walked over and admired the beginnings of a round black figure with stick legs and a spiral tail. "Is that Benny?"

The little girl nodded. "Benny is going to a pig resort," she said to Amy.

He hasn't told her yet. Melissa bent to give her a hug. "I'll see you later."

She drove back to the farm rather than going directly to the grocery store, so she could consult with Diane first. All along the narrow winding road, she found her thoughts bouncing from Alice Ann to Gregory to Diane and back to Gregory. *Gregory, Gregory.* Penetrating dark eyes, knowing smile. That arched black brow. Those *shoulders.* He was too old for her, she reminded herself. Too staid and serious. And yet she liked that about him, too. He was responsible. Reliable. Strong.

He wasn't someone she could twist around her finger. Oh, no, he was far too sharp for that. She was probably a fool, trying to hide Diane and her kids on his property. Why couldn't he have been some bumbling farmer whose mind worked as slowly as cows ambling across a pasture? Instead, he looked as if he could see straight into her brain and read her thoughts. Luckily, they *weren't* telepathic.

She chuckled, recalling the cricket bat. She didn't need telepathy to know where *his* mind had been at that minute.

Back at the farm, Melissa parked outside the cottage. She knocked, then pushed open the door. Diane and her kids were sitting in the dark among all the furniture, looking bleary-eyed after their third night here.

"Gregory and Alice Ann are gone," Melissa said. "Come up to the house. You can shower and have something to eat."

"May I wash our clothes?" Diane asked.

"Of course," she replied. "We've got three hours until Alice Ann comes back."

The woman, the boy and the little girl emerged from the dark cottage into the brilliant sunlight, blinking and stretching their limbs. Diane clutched a toiletry bag and clean clothes. Callie stared at the weaner pigs, which rushed to the fence, curious to see the humans go by. Maxie danced around Josh, wagging her tail and barking. Josh picked up a fallen pinecone and threw it for the dog. Maxie fetched it back and the pair played the game all the way to the house.

Melissa found them all towels and let them use her room to change. While they were cleaning up, she made breakfast. Starting with Callie, then Josh, the trio emerged in fresh clothes, the children's faces scrubbed shiny and pink. Josh's short red hair stood up in tufts, and Callie's long, reddish blond hair curled at the ends with the damp. The bruises on her face were gradually changing from deep purple to reddish brown.

Diane had styled her streaked blond hair using Melissa's hair dryer, and although her casual pants and fine cotton knit top were slightly wrinkled, they were clean. "I don't think I've ever enjoyed a shower more!" she said. "After breakfast could you get out your first-aid kit? I should change Josh's bandage."

They all sat down to eat scrambled eggs and toast. "My specialty," Melissa joked. "It's about the only thing I can cook."

"They're great!" Josh said, tucking in.

"Mmm," Callie agreed with her mouth full.

When they were finished, Melissa went out to her car and brought in the kit. She leaned against the counter and watched as Diane removed the old bandage, wet from his shower and starting to peel off. When his mom touched an antiseptic swab to the wound, Josh winced and cried out.

Melissa moved to his side and stroked his forehead, keeping her gaze averted from the gash, which oozed droplets of fresh blood. "Look, Maxie's waiting to play with you." It was true. The dog sat on the floor in front of Josh, watching expectantly.

"Hey, Maxie," Josh said, holding out his hand for Maxie to lick his fingers.

Melissa kept on talking quietly to Josh while his mother applied a new dressing. Gradually, the unsettled feeling in her stomach calmed down.

Finally Diane rose and went to wash her hands. "All done. Josh, you can go play with Maxie now." To Melissa, she said, "Thanks. He's such a squirmer, but you managed to get him to sit still."

Melissa shrugged that away. "What you do is wonderful. It must be so satisfying to be a nurse and be able to make people better."

"I loved it," Diane admitted. "I never should have given it up."

"Doesn't the blood ever bother you?"

She laughed. "You get used to it. You should try it. You'd make a great nurse."

"I wish. But I'd never be able to stomach it. I'm going to be an architect or something Really Big." Melissa held out her hand. "Could you take a look at my thumb? It's pretty sore."

Diane gently prodded the swollen digit. Melissa winced. "It's a bit inflamed." Diane dabbed on antiseptic and wrapped the finger in a Band-Aid. "There you go."

"That's all?"

"Try not to pick at it."

"Great. Super." Melissa smoothed the edge of the Band-Aid down. "You said you could help me plan meals? Can we make a shopping list?"

"Certainly," Diane said, clearing the table. "While you're getting groceries I'll cook a dinner with whatever's in the pantry, something that you can heat up later."

"If you make extra you can have a hot meal for lunch and make sandwiches for dinner," Melissa suggested, going to the sideboard for the yellow legal pad Gregory kept there.

"Can we have lollies?" Callie asked.

"And potato chips?" Josh called from the veranda.

"We're not at home," Diane said. "We can't afford junk food. Now, please take your dirty clothes and towel to the laundry room. You, too, Callie."

"There are clothes already in the machine," Melissa said, rising. "I'll get them out."

"Don't bother. I'll wash those, as well." Diane started to clear the table. "I'll clean up the house while you're at the store."

"I don't know what I'm going to do when you leave," Melissa said. "The house will be a disaster, we'll be eating canned soup and Gregory won't have a clue why."

"I wish I knew when we'll be able to leave," Diane fretted.

"I'll keep trying to find out when Constance is coming home." Melissa bent to the task of making a grocery list. "Coffee, peanut butter…"

"Milk," Diane added, checking the fridge. "Cheese…"

GREGORY'S TEN-THIRTY CLIENTS were Bob and Ruth Whitmore, sheep graziers in their sixties who'd gotten him to put their ten-thousand-hectare property into a living trust for their children: two sons and a daughter. Bob was lean and weathered, Ruth round and comfortable, and both had a stoicism that came from a lifetime on the land.

Gregory produced a document and showed them the pages tagged for their signatures. While they signed, he swiveled his chair around to gaze out the window. Even though it was a weekday and past the summer-holiday period, tourists still strolled the wide boulevard. Some sat at the outdoor cafés.

Melissa's apple-green Volkswagen tootled past.

Gregory sat up straight, conscious of a buzz in his veins. He got up and went closer to the window to watch her turn left at the end of the block. She must be going to the grocery store.

"That's the lot," Bob announced. "We've signed our life away."

Gregory returned to his seat and glanced over each page. "I'll have copies made and sent out to you."

"Thanks, Gregory," Bob said.

"Stop by sometime," Ruth added. "And bring that cute little girl of yours. I see her at the play school sometimes when I drop off my granddaughter, Tammy."

Gregory walked the Whitmores out and shook hands, bidding them farewell. Once they'd gone he went to the reception desk to speak to Louise, a woman in her fifties who'd been with the firm for over twenty-five years. "When's my next appointment? I thought I'd nick out to the shop."

Louise consulted the book. "Not till eleven, but Peter Abernathy called, asking if his mortgage documents were ready."

"They're on my desk," Gregory said. "I'll be back in a few minutes."

He made his escape and strode down the street, telling himself he simply needed to remind Melissa which brand of coffee he liked. While he was in the store he would pick up something for lunch. Yes, good plan.

The grocery store was populated by mothers with small children, tourists and senior citizens. Gregory picked out an apple and moved to the deli, where he ordered a hot meat pie in a foil wrapper. He made a circuit of the fresh-food sections, glancing down each aisle as he passed.

He found Melissa in confectionary. Her back was to him but her long red hair was unmistakable. Although he liked her in skirts, she was no less feminine in those figure-hugging jeans. Slowing his pace, he casually strolled toward her. "Melissa."

She spun to face him, clutching a bag of individually wrapped milk chocolate koalas. "Gregory! I didn't expect to see you here."

"I, uh, came to pick up something for lunch." He held up his meat pie and apple as evidence, then nodded at the chocolate. "If those are for Alice Ann, she'll only give them to Benny."

"No, they're for…me." Melissa laughed guiltily as she tossed them into her shopping trolley. "I'm afraid I've got a sweet tooth."

His gaze followed the bag. The cart was piled high with food. "Are you expecting a nuclear winter I haven't heard about?"

"I beg your pardon?" Her fingers toyed with her earring, a cascade of tiny amethyst and jade beads.

"All that food," he said, nodding at it. "You've got enough there to feed a family of six."

"A family of six!" Melissa laughed a little too loudly and long. "That's funny."

He cocked one eyebrow. "No one's ever accused me of being humorous."

That earned him a genuine smile. "Well, if you're ever charged with perpetrating a joke, I know a good lawyer."

"You mean, *you* won't defend me?"

"To the death," she said lightly, and started down the aisle. "You haven't told Alice Ann about Benny yet, have you?"

"Ah, no," he admitted. "I will soon, though. The longer I leave it, the harder it'll be."

"I've been thinking about this and I don't think you should tell her," Melissa said. "I've got a plan."

Gregory moved to the side to let another shopper past. "This I've got to hear."

"You let her go on thinking the pigs are going to a resort. Then when Benny's been away for a few months—a long time to a kid—you tell her he's gone on a cruise to Hawaii."

"That's as bad as a pig resort," he said as they turned the corner into the next aisle. "I don't want to lie."

"You've already lied," she reminded him.

"I didn't. Alice Ann jumped to conclusions."

"You didn't correct her," Melissa pointed out. "If she still pines for Benny after six months, you tell her he got a rare pig disease and died." Melissa consulted the shopping list in her hand and loaded half a dozen large tins of tomatoes in her trolley. "You can give him a fabulous imaginary funeral, with Hawaiian princesses carrying his coffin on their shoulders as they wind their way up the volcano to fling his body into the smoking crater. Alice Ann would cry, but she'd be comforted by the beautiful last rites."

"You're completely out of your mind—you realize that, don't you?" Gregory picked up a jar of marinated artichokes and added it to her cart.

"You should think about it," Melissa said. "You don't want to traumatize Alice Ann. She's very sensitive."

"Do you think I don't know that about my own daughter?" he said mildly. "Do you think I don't worry about her every night and day?"

Melissa stopped at the end of the aisle near a checkout and met his gaze. "I know you do."

Gregory, held by the warmth in her eyes, smiled

at her foolishly until the meat pie burning his palm brought him back to his senses. He transferred the pie to the other hand. "Are you ready to come through the checkout? I'll put that on my credit card."

"Uh, no. I've still got a few more things to get." Melissa fiddled with one beaded earring, glancing away.

"You're not buying pork, I hope. We've got a freezer full of—"

Her attention had been caught by a rack of newspapers. She picked one up and glanced at the headlines.

"Anything interesting?" Gregory asked, peering over her shoulder. "I haven't had time to watch the news or read a paper in days."

Melissa folded the newspaper and stuffed it into the trolley. "Just the usual." She moved on toward the next aisle. "By the way, have you heard from Constance?"

"No," he replied, surprised she would ask. "Have you?"

Melissa shook her head, watching him closely. "But then, she's never been a great communicator."

"You think not? I find that odd, considering she's a retired journalist."

"I mean, with her *friends.*" Melissa started to move away. "I'd better finish before the ice cream melts."

"Sure. Well, I'll see you tonight." He started to walk away, then turned around. "What are you planning to make for dinner?"

"Dinner?" Her blue eyes widened as if she'd forgotten she had a mountain of food in her trolley. "Why, that's going to be a surprise."

CHAPTER SEVEN

THE WELCOMING AROMA of home-cooked food curled into Gregory's nostrils as he came through the door that night. Melissa and Alice Ann were at the kitchen table, talking quietly as they exchanged crayons and admired each other's coloring. The kitchen sink gleamed and the floor had been washed. Clean laundry, ironed and folded, sat in the basket on a chair, ready to be taken to the bedrooms. Inside him, a sense of order and peace unfurled.

Gregory came into the room and dropped his briefcase on the sideboard. "Hello, you two."

At the sound of his voice Alice Ann raised her head. Her gauze wings caught on the back of the chair as she scrambled down and ran to greet him. "Daddy!"

Gregory lifted her into his arms. "How's my girl? What are you, a butterfly?"

"No, silly, I'm a fairy princess! Melissa and me are coloring."

"So I see." He nodded to Melissa, who looked

fresh and young with a tiara nestled in her rich red hair. How did she cook and clean all day and still look as though she hadn't lifted a finger? "Something smells good."

Melissa selected another crayon for her cartoon drawing of a Wessex Saddleback pig. "That would be dinner."

He couldn't decide if her smile was mischievous, seductive, innocent or a bit of all three. "Is it still a surprise?"

"I'll give you a hint," she said. "It's a casserole."

She was teasing him. "What kind?"

"The delicious kind." She jumped up and looked at the oven timer. "It'll be ready in twenty minutes."

"Time enough for me to check on the pigs," he said. "Want to help, Alice Ann?"

"I'm going to help Melissa set the table. Look at the collar she made for Benny." Alice Ann held up a spangled cloth collar in red and blue. "It even gots extra snaps so it's adjustabubble."

Melissa started packing the crayons in their box. "We'll try it on him tomorrow."

Gregory changed out of his suit and into jeans and a lightweight pullover. The early autumn days were still warm, but come evening it started to cool down. With Maxie at his heels, he left the house and headed for the barn. Gregory enjoyed getting out of doors and stretching his legs on his daily round. Today he checked the water troughs to make sure they were full and that the automatic tap hadn't clogged or jammed. As he walked the paddocks, he scanned the fences for breaks in the wire mesh and saw that a section between the weaners' area and the boar's enclosure had been torn away from the post. He would need to fix that this weekend so the boar couldn't get in with the other pigs. One of these days he'd have to segregate the old man completely.

Then there was the cottage, another thing that required his attention. He could hire someone to clear out all that old furniture, but he wanted to look it over himself, to see if there was anything he could use in the house. The owners had gone to England for three months, then written him to say they were staying indefinitely and to dispose of the furniture as he pleased.

He found Ruthie in her corner nest, which was well padded with torn-up grass and the odd plastic bag she'd found blown into the paddock. Her big floppy ears covered her eyes and her swollen sides gently heaved. She was, indeed, close to popping, as Melissa put it.

Melissa. In spite of his initial reservations, she'd turned out to be every bit as efficient and capable as she'd promised. Her presence added something important to his home that had been missing.

Sugar and spice and everything nice.

He couldn't let himself start thinking along those lines. She was Alice Ann's nanny, not a potential girlfriend. Nor did he want a girlfriend; he wanted a wife, someone to build a life with. But she'd have to be the right person for him. Melissa was an attractive woman, but she seemed flighty, unpredictable. Take the way she'd suddenly applied for the job after telling him the day before she wasn't a nanny. Now that was impulsive. He hoped she wouldn't decide just as suddenly and unexpectedly that she no longer wanted the job.

Gregory turned away from the fence. Something glittery in the dirt caught his eye. He bent down and picked up a child's hair clip. Made of sparkly pink plastic, it was shaped like a butterfly. He put it in his pocket to give back to Alice Ann.

Whistling for Maxie, Gregory headed for the house. By the time he'd washed up, Melissa had dinner on the table. Gregory served himself a helping of the casserole after Melissa and Alice Ann had taken theirs. "What did you say this was?"

Melissa took a bite. "Beef." She chewed some more. "Beef with wine and mushrooms. Boeuf Bourguignonne. Wow!" she added quietly.

"Wine!" Alice Ann exclaimed. "I'm too young to drink."

"Don't do any driving," Melissa teased. "The police might pull you over."

Gregory took a bite of stew. The meat was tender and flavorful, a huge improvement on his cooking. "This is excellent."

"Thank you." Melissa's eyes were demurely cast down.

"I noticed you cleaned up the house, too."

She shrugged modestly. "It's my job."

"Daddy, why is the sky blue?" Alice Ann asked.

"That's a good question," Gregory said. "There's a scientific explanation but I can't remember it right now. We'll look it up after dinner."

"Do you know, Melissa?" Alice Ann asked.

"Because blue is a pretty color?" Melissa suggested with a wink for Gregory.

"I know!" Alice Ann exclaimed. "Maybe angels stand on clouds and dip their wings into big pots of blue paint, then fly across the sky, painting it blue."

"Maybe," Melissa said, laughing. "And when the sun goes down they dip their wings in red and pink."

Gregory smiled. Melissa was good for Alice Ann; he was too serious sometimes. He remembered the hair clip and took it out of his pocket. "You dropped this outside."

Alice Ann looked at it. "That's not mine."

"It must be."

"It's not," she insisted.

"How can you be sure? You've been given so many hair accessories by your grandmother and your aunts that you probably don't remember half of what you own."

"Melissa and me went through all my hair stuff today looking for a yellow hair clip to go with my wings. That wasn't in the box." As she turned it over in her hand, her expression became dreamy. "Maybe it belongs to another little girl... Cinderella. She lives in the cottage all by herself, with only mice and spiders for friends. At night when the moon is full, she comes out to play."

Melissa fumbled with her fork, which clattered against her plate. Retrieving it, she clutched it tightly. "Goodness, you do have an imagination. You know there's no one living in the cottage."

The child frowned and stuck her bottom lip out. "It's not mine, so it must belong to someone else."

"You haven't had any friends over lately. Whose could it be but yours?" Gregory argued.

"Let *me* see," Melissa said, reaching for the clip. She laughed. "Why, this is mine." She took a curl and clipped it off her forehead beneath her tiara.

Alice Ann giggled. "You look funny!"

Gregory cracked a smile. She looked cute and sexy. He'd have thought the clip was a child's, but then, he wouldn't put anything past Melissa. "Mystery solved."

"Daddy, can I be 'scused?" Alice Ann asked. "I want to go play with my barn animals."

"Go ahead. Melissa?" Gregory touched her arm to stop her from leaving. She looked up, startled. Swiftly, he removed his hand and cleared his throat. "We neglected to talk about something during your interview—how long you're going to be here."

Melissa put her hands in her lap. "I thought we'd just take it month to month."

"I'd prefer a definite arrangement for a longer

term," Gregory said. "Alice Ann needs continuity in her life."

"*You're* her continuity," Melissa pointed out.

"True, but she spends many hours of the day exclusively with the nanny. Already, she's attached to you. The sudden departure of another significant figure in her life could be traumatic."

"How long were you thinking of? And did you…" Melissa bit her lip. "Did you want it in writing?"

"I could draw up a contract if you prefer, but I don't think that's necessary. I trust you." She grimaced at that. Was he embarrassing her? "Ideally, I'd like you to commit to, say, a year."

"A year!" Melissa shook her head. "I don't know. I adore Alice Ann, but a year is a long time. You might decide well before then that I'm a hopeless ditz."

He laughed. "Why do you run yourself down? This is only your first day and already you've cleaned the whole house and cooked a spectacular meal. Alice Ann is happier than I've seen her in months. I must admit I had reservations at first, but you've convinced me you're ideal." He paused. "Or have you decided already you don't want to stay?"

"No, it's not that," she said slowly. "Do you remember when I told you I wanted to do Something Big? I enjoy looking after children and I do believe it's important. *Very* important. But I also want to start a formal career."

Gregory leaned back in his chair. So looking after Alice Ann was a stopgap. He should have known Melissa was too good to be true. And yet the part of him that wasn't bound up in self-interest applauded her ambition. "What kind of a career, may I ask?"

"I don't know yet."

"If it's a matter of having time off to go to classes or study, we could arrange something."

"You're very generous," she said uncomfortably.

"Plus there's no need for you to stay through the weekend. You're allowed to have a life of your own. Friends, family…" He trailed off, unwilling to add *boyfriend*. Which was ridiculous, since he'd only just met her and she was too flighty for him, anyway.

"Speaking of family and time off," she began. "It's my birthday on Saturday and I'll be going to a party at my sister's house."

"That's fine."

"As for moving out on weekends, I'd rather not," she told him. "My parents are wonderful people, but they're always trying to meddle in my life. If I'm at home they'd have access to me 24-7."

Gregory nodded, trying not to reveal his satisfaction at knowing she wanted to live full-time at the farm. Although if he was smart, he'd be concentrating on getting her *out* of the farmhouse. Making a sudden decision, he added, "I'll take tomorrow afternoon off to clear out the cottage for you. Rain is forecast for sometime in the next day or two, and I'd like to get this done before that."

"Tomorrow afternoon? So soon." She clasped her hands tightly together. "Wonderful."

Gregory studied the tense smile that belied her words. Was it possible she was enjoying their close proximity, too? He'd thought he detected a certain tendency for her gaze to linger on his... No, this was foolish wishful thinking. Even if she *was* attracted, she'd just told him she couldn't commit to anything long-term. And besides, he was too *old*. She wanted to do something with her life, and the fact that she didn't know what just made her future more uncertain.

"So how long would you feel comfortable agreeing to?" he asked, getting back to the subject. "Six months?"

"Two?" she suggested.

"Four?"

"Three?"

Gregory knew when to quit. "Sold."

When the time was up, he'd just have to find a way to convince her to stay longer.

"I TRIED TO PRESS Gregory about where Constance is and when she's coming home, but I didn't get very far," Melissa told Diane as they walked past the weaners' paddock the next morning on their way to collect eggs from Constance's henhouse. In her blue jeans and boots, with a basket slung over her arm, Melissa was feeling pleasantly bucolic. "Gregory did say he wouldn't have expected to hear from her while she's away. I wonder if that's because she's overseas or because they're not very close."

"Constance usually sends me a postcard when she goes away," Diane said. "I haven't received one this time, unless it's come since we've been gone." She glanced around nervously, as she did whenever she was out in the open. "Stay close when we're outside, kids. You never know when someone might come up the lane."

"Did you read the newspaper report?" Melissa asked. "There's a state-wide search for you. The missing wife of a prominent judge is big news."

"Did Gregory see the paper?" Diane asked.

"I gave the one I bought straight to you. I don't know if he read one at work, but I don't think so. I made sure he didn't watch the evening news by strategically putting dinner on the table at the same time. He sets great store in sitting down to a proper family meal every night."

"That's nice," Diane said. "James always worked late. To tell you the truth, I used to be relieved when he wasn't home and the kids and I could have a relaxed dinner."

They came to the paddock enclosing the boar. He stood alone on top of a mound of dirt, his yellow tusks curving viciously out of his bottom jaw. When he saw them he grunted. Warning them off, Melissa was quite certain.

"Can I go in and pat him?" Josh asked. "He looks lonely."

"Oh. no," Melissa said, hurrying on, "that pig would trample you with his little cloven hooves."

"I'm not afraid of him!" the boy replied scornfully.

"I am," Melissa said. "I had a nasty encounter with a boar as a child."

"What happened?" Callie asked, skipping to keep up.

"Let's just say I still bear the scars."

"Let's see," Josh said, interested.

"They're emotional scars," Melissa explained. "But no less painful."

They came to the end of the paddock and crossed the lane to Constance's. As the two women started through the apple orchard, the children ran ahead, Callie to gather windfalls, Josh to scramble up the nearest tree.

"Stay in the orchard," Diane told them. "We'll just be a few minutes."

"They seem happy, considering their situation," Melissa said. "Kids are amazingly resilient."

"They're handling it very well," Diane agreed. "They're missing school, but Callie's practicing her reading and I brought Josh's arithmetic book."

Outside the chicken coop, in the fenced pen, big brown hens were scratching in the dust and clucking softly. Diane climbed the short flight of rough-hewn wooden steps and ducked inside. Melissa followed. A double row of wooden poles stretched the width of the coop, for the chickens to roost on at night. In a waist-high wooden trough filled with straw a lone hen was sitting on a nest. She fluffed her feathers and clucked indignantly.

"That one's hatching a clutch of eggs," Diane said. "We'll leave her alone."

Dust motes danced in the slices of light coming through the cracks between the boards. The odor of straw and chicken droppings wasn't totally unpleasant.

"Gregory should get chickens," Melissa said as she peered into the trough and found two smooth brown eggs stuck with bits of downy feather nestled in the straw. She placed them in her basket. "This is cool."

"It hasn't really sunk in for Josh and Callie that we've left," Diane said, returning to the subject of her kids. "When they get tired they want their own things around them. I hope I've made the right choice. And that they don't blame me for tearing them away from their old life."

Melissa could imagine Diane's beautiful house and the children's playroom, complete with all the material goodies James's well-paying career could provide. Such a life would be financially secure and socially desirable. She was struck by the enormity of what Diane had done in running away with no money and two small children.

"I think you're very brave," she said. "You're a good mother doing her best to protect her children. You might be short of money now, but you're trained as a nurse, so you'll be able to support them. So what if they don't have their toys for a while? The most important thing is they still have you."

Diane slipped another three eggs into the basket. When she glanced up, her eyes were moist. "Thank you. I needed someone to remind me." She paused. "You must be wondering why I even married a man like James."

Melissa reached into the straw and felt a little thrill when she discovered two more eggs. This was better than an Easter-egg hunt. "I presume you didn't know what he was like until it was too late."

"If I had I would never have said yes," she explained. "At first I liked his take-charge attitude. He involved himself in every aspect of my life. I thought he was fascinated by me. In reality, he was controlling. I mistook that for love." She gave Melissa a shamefaced smile. "Pretty pathetic and stupid, huh?"

Melissa set down the basket and gave her a quick hug. "You don't expect someone who tells you they love you to abuse your trust. You're not stupid. You're a survivor. A fighter. Everything's going to be all right now. You're going to take care of yourself."

Diane smiled, blinking. "Yes, you're right. I'm going to be fine. I'm actually looking forward to going back to nursing." She glanced around. "I guess we're done."

Melissa hoisted the basket of eggs onto her hip

and followed Diane out. "We need to feed the hens, too. Gregory says Constance keeps the pellets in that storage shed."

"That's right. I've seen her get them out many times."

They walked over to the corrugated-iron shed next to the garage. Inside was a large plastic garbage can with a bucket sitting on the lid. Melissa scooped pellets into the bucket and carried it back to the pen, squeezing inside when Diane opened the gate for her. The hens hurried forward, cluck ing in anticipation. Melissa poured the feed into a wide shallow pan and left the chickens pecking furiously.

"That's done," she said with satisfaction, watching them eat. "Thanks, girls. See you tomorrow."

She turned to go, casting her gaze skyward to see if the rain Gregory had said was predicted was on its way. Clouds were massing in a dark front to the east, but they looked far away. "Gregory's taking this afternoon off. He's going to clear out the cottage."

"Oh, dear!" Diane said. "I suppose we could hide in the chicken coop, but it's so messy underfoot we wouldn't be able to sit down…. There's always the woods…but if it starts raining we'll get soaked."

"Don't panic," Melissa said, thinking hard. "I might have a way to stall him."

CHAPTER EIGHT

"MY EX-WIFE HASN'T LET ME see my kids in three weeks," Bill Powell told Gregory. The big man rubbed his palms on his grease-stained mechanic's overalls. "Annie and Tim, they don't know how much I want to be with them."

Gregory knew all too well what it was like for a man to be deprived of his child by a vindictive woman. Consulting Bill's file, he said, "You're supposed to have your children one full day on the weekend and one overnight stay during the week."

"You don't need to tell me." His client's hands curled into fists on his thighs. "Teri's always got some bloody excuse—Annie has a birthday party to go to or Tim's sick. Or they're just plain not there when I go to pick them up!"

"Have you been keeping up your support payments?"

"In full, on time, every fortnight. And I always bring the kids back exactly when I'm supposed to."

"Your ex-wife is clearly not complying with the

family court order," Gregory stated. "We could try mediation again—"

"No," Bill said. "We had an agreement and she broke it. It's time to get tough."

He nodded. "I agree. I'll speak to her lawyer. We won't let this happen again."

The mechanic pushed himself to his feet. "Thanks, Gregory. Why is it that women get all the breaks when it comes to custody? It's like men don't have any rights at all."

"My job is to make sure you're not deprived of your right to see your children," Gregory assured him. "It's a responsibility I take very seriously."

Bill shook his hand. "I appreciate it."

After his client left, Gregory made the call to Teri Powell's lawyer. It wasn't fair that a good man like Bill Powell should lose contact with his children. Gregory knew that frustration and anguish. If Debra had lived he might still be fighting for the right to see Alice Ann.

Sighing heavily, he swiveled around to check the weather. Clouds were gathering to the east, but elsewhere the sky was a perfect blue. He glanced at his watch. Just after midday. Melissa would have picked up Alice Ann and be on her way back to the farm. If he left now he'd get home in time to have lunch with them before he tackled the cottage.

Gregory picked up the phone and called Louise. "Just a reminder that I'll be leaving for the day in a few minutes, so don't book any appointments for me this afternoon."

"Someone is on the way to your office right now," Louise said. "She insisted you'd want to see her. She's got Alice Ann with her."

"Melissa?" Gregory heard a knock and glanced up.

"That would be me." She sauntered into his office looking like a slice of summer in a lime-green sleeveless dress and oversize sunglasses.

"Daddy!" Alice Ann ran in ahead of her. Long brown locks had escaped from her hair tie, and she brushed them back impatiently. "Look what I drawed."

Gregory pulled her onto his knee and studied her drawing. It appeared to be some kind of animal, but which way was up? "I may be going out on a limb here but…is that Benny wearing his new collar?"

"Yes!" Alice Ann beamed at him.

"An excellent likeness!" Gregory cast Melissa a glance and was rewarded with an approving smile. "What brings you two here?"

"We're going on a picnic and we want you to come," Alice Ann told him, scrambling off his lap.

"I was going to clean out the cottage this afternoon before it rains," he said. "Going for a picnic is way too much fun for a lawyer to have in the middle of the day."

"Don't be silly," Melissa said firmly. "You hired

me so you'd have more quality time with Alice Ann, right?"

"Yes, but—"

"The rain is predicted for early afternoon. You won't have time to clean out the cottage, anyway."

"I could make a start—"

"You *will* have time for a picnic. You work too much. You need to enjoy yourself more."

Gregory leaned back in his chair, amused. "Were you this assertive when I hired you?"

"Come on, Daddy," Alice Ann begged. *"Please!"*

"Oh, I suppose another day won't hurt." He reached for his jacket on the back of the chair. "Let's go."

FROM THE Wombat Hill Botanical Garden they could see the approaching storm chasing shadows across the undulating farmland. But here on the sloping lawn, dotted with trees from all over the world, the dark clouds seemed far off.

Gregory carried the picnic basket to where Melissa was spreading a blanket beneath an enormous Chinese ginkgo. While she unpacked the food he unbuttoned his jacket and eased himself down. "This was a good idea."

"Take off your shoes," Melissa suggested. "Feel the grass between your toes." Her toenails were painted a bright red to match her belt and sandals.

"Come on, Daddy." Alice Ann unbuckled her own sturdy sandals. "We're all going barefoot."

Gregory unlaced his shoes and took them off. His socks followed, leaving his pale feet looking oddly vulnerable beneath his suit pants. Sure enough, the grass felt cool and soothing. He took off his tie, folded it and put it in his pocket. That felt so good he undid the buttons on his cuffs and rolled up his sleeves. He felt himself start to relax. Definitely, this was a fine idea.

Melissa handed him a container of sandwiches. Gregory took one and bit into it, savoring the robust flavors of roast beef and sharp mustard. "How did you know this is my favorite?"

"We're telepathic, remember?" Dappled sunlight played over Melissa's bare shoulders. She wore another pair of dangly earrings, a confection of crimson beads and crystals. She was the most exquisitely feminine woman Gregory had ever met, from the delicate angles of her cheekbones to her soft, tapered fingers with their perfectly shaped nails buffed to a soft natural shine.

Sandwich in hand, Alice Ann pushed herself to her feet and headed toward a nearby flower bed, where yellow wings fluttered above a clump of scented blossoms. "I'm going to catch a butterfly."

Melissa reached for another sandwich. Without thinking, Gregory took her hand and ran his thumb across the soft smooth skin. Melissa went very still, as if she was holding her breath. Gregory's fingers slid around to her inner wrist, drawn like a magnet by the throbbing pulse, which seemed to speed up at his touch. He heard her quick indrawn breath.

"Sorry." He let go of her hand. "That was highly inappropriate." Clearing his throat, he added, "I was merely wondering how you keep your hands in such good condition with all that house cleaning."

"Gloves." Her voice cracked as she rubbed her wrist with her other hand. Then she repeated the word more steadily. "Gloves of all kinds. Rubber for the dishes, leather for yard work, white cotton for overnight after I've rubbed lotion into my hands."

Gregory thrust away an image of her wearing white cotton gloves and nothing else. He searched for a safe topic. "You never did tell me how you know Constance."

"Um…" Melissa hesitated so long he stopped eating and waited. Finally she said, "Mutual friends. She used to live next door to a friend of mine in Ballarat."

The explanation was plausible enough, but the way she wouldn't meet his gaze made him wonder if she was telling the truth. That first day she'd come up his lane she'd acted strangely, too. Did she really know his neighbor? He was beginning to think not. Melissa never mentioned Constance's trip, even though it was a source of great interest and speculation to those who knew her.

"I hope her holiday turns out to be everything it's cracked up to be," he said, fishing for a slipup.

Melissa threw a scrap of bread to a kookaburra eyeing them from a branch of the ginkgo. The breeze ruffled the cream feathers on the bird's comically large head. A blue flash glinted on its spread wings as it swooped to pluck the bread out of the grass.

"Constance was really excited about going," she replied, without looking at him. Her slender fingers shredded the remainder of her sandwich. "She bought a whole new wardrobe. She never stopped talking about it. She couldn't wait."

Gregory raised his eyebrows. Constance would hardly have needed a new wardrobe. And although she'd been determined to see the expedition through, she had only agreed to it because her cousin from America wanted to go. "Constance told *me* she was terrified."

"She *was* a tad apprehensive." Melissa backtracked quickly, throwing the last of her sandwich to the kookaburra.

She didn't have a clue about Constance. Gregory had an idea why Melissa was lying, but continued the charade to see what else she would say. "I imagine she's pretty sore right about now."

Melissa threw him a quick glance and laughed nervously. "Oh, yeah, she would be."

"But she'll take it in her stride." He noted Melissa's growing agitation. Really, he shouldn't toy with her.

"She's an adventurous woman," Melissa asserted.

Gregory was silent. Constance was a homebody, no more adventurous than one of his pigs. "You don't actually know her, do you?"

The sun dimmed as a cloud passed in front. In a very small voice, Melissa said, "No."

"I know why you're lying," he said gently. "You can't fool me."

"You do? I can't?" She looked stricken, terrified, even as her words came tumbling out. "I'm *so* sorry. I used you. I know it was wrong, but I just had to."

He held up a hand to stem the rush. "It's okay. Others have tried the same thing."

Melissa went still and looked at him sideways. "They have?"

"Constance's eggs are the cheapest around," he said. "I don't blame you for pretending to know her to get them."

Melissa's whole body seemed to go limp. "H-how did you guess?"

"Constance wrote me out a list of her regular customers," he said simply. "You weren't on it." He paused and said very seriously, "You can admit the rest now."

"The rest?" she squeaked.

"You know what I'm talking about."

"I do?" Her shoulders had tensed again and she gripped her hands together.

"Taking the nanny job so you could have unfettered access to all the eggs you can eat."

She stared at him in stunned silence, then exploded. "Why, that's ridiculous! Who would do that? I wanted the nanny position because… because Alice Ann is adorable. Because I needed a job and because it was convenient to have another place to live besides my parents' house." She paused in her headlong rush for breath. "Is that enough? How many reasons do I need?"

Gregory grinned. "I'm teasing."

"Why you…" Planting both hands on his chest, she shoved him onto his back, then loomed over him like a very sexy avenging Fury.

She was right, a picnic was just what he'd needed. He couldn't remember when he'd enjoyed himself so much. Gregory gripped her wrists, holding her in position. "Now what are you going to do with me?"

"I'm going to—" Whatever she'd been about to say was drowned out by a clap of thunder directly overhead. The clouds that had been building burst open, releasing rain in a near-solid sheet of water. It obscured the trees and soaked Gregory and Melissa in moments. Alice Ann came running back, her hair plastered to her head and her dress sopping wet. Melissa quickly packed the leftover food into the basket and gathered up the blanket. Gregory grabbed both and they ran to Melissa's Volkswagen.

Inside, the windows steamed up. Rain battered the roof so loudly it seemed to Gregory it was inside his skull. Melissa's thin dress clung to her wet skin and rain beaded on her shoulders. A drop of water slid off her chin, landed on her collarbone and slid between her breasts.

"Are you angry with me?" she asked, her low voice almost drowned out by the driving rain.

"Huh?" He lifted his gaze. How could he be angry when all he could think about was kissing her? Gregory glanced into the backseat at Alice Ann. She was drawing pigs in the condensation on the window and humming to herself. Gregory turned back to Melissa. "I *should* be angry. Mostly I'm disappointed and confused. Lying about knowing Constance seems so pointless."

Melissa stared straight ahead at the streaming windshield, her forehead furrowed. Finally she turned to him, all contrition gone. "So lying for a good reason would be acceptable?"

"Who's the lawyer here?" he demanded. "Tell you what, I'll forgive you if you tell me the real reason you took the job as Alice Ann's nanny."

She shifted her gaze. "I told you already."

"I place great importance on honesty." His glance flicked to his daughter, aware there was an element of hypocrisy in his position. "Certain issues notwithstanding."

Melissa inclined her head. "I accept that, up to a point." Meaning Alice Ann.

Gregory kept his eyes on her. "If you want to tell me anything else, now would be a good time."

"Actually—" She broke off as a shiver convulsed her shoulders. Goose bumps dotted her arms.

"You're cold." He reached into the backseat for his suit jacket. Ignoring her protests, he slid the jacket around her shoulders and tugged it closed.

"Thank you." She blew a wisp of wet hair out of her eyes and regarded him with a soft smile. "You are a really nice man." With a quick glance at Alice Ann, still absorbed in drawing on the window, she leaned forward and kissed him lightly on the lips, lingering a moment, leaving her scent and her touch behind.

He blinked. The next thing he knew, Melissa was turning the key in the ignition.

"Wait a minute," he said. "What were you going to say just then?"

She threw him an oblique look, at once vulnerable and mysterious. "Nothing. Nothing at all."

MELISSA DROPPED GREGORY off at his office where he said he had a change of clothes. There was no point in him going home if he couldn't work on the cottage. She drove back to the house through the teeming rain, winding through the towering gums closely lining the road. In the backseat, Alice Ann sang softly as she played a game with her plastic farm animals.

Annoyed with herself, Melissa thumped the steering wheel. She'd had the perfect opportunity to ask Gregory when Constance was coming home, and she'd blown it. He'd rattled her so much with that serious look of his, and his softly spoken interrogation. *Is there anything else you want to tell me?*

Let's see, she could tell him she was hiding a runaway woman and her two children in his cottage. Or she could mention that he was the most attractive man she'd ever met. Compared to Gregory, Julio seemed like a boy.

What she wished she could say was that she was sorry she was lying to him and that someday he'd realize it was for a good cause.

Why on earth had she kissed him? At the time, she'd told herself it was a way to distract him. But the moment her mouth had touched his, her blood had started to fizz and the tingling sensation had spread from her lips right through to the tips of her toes. That kiss had less to do with distraction than it had with the attraction she'd been fighting since she'd met him. What a fool she was! The pressure of his mouth, the heat of his fingers against her wet skin, the steamy beat of the rain over the pounding of her heart would be imprinted on her brain forever.

Alarm bells were ringing so loudly in her head she was surprised Alice Ann wasn't asking what the noise was. A kiss like that could only lead in one direction. Fibbing to him as the nanny was bad enough, but lying to him as a lover would be a whole lot more serious.

If she told him about Diane, would he understand? Or would he fire her and never want to see her again? It wasn't about *her*, Melissa reminded herself. She couldn't tell Diane's secret without her permission.

A sneeze from the backseat pulled her gaze to the rearview mirror. "Are you cold, sweetie?"

"No," Alice Ann said, and sneezed again.

"We'll be home soon and get you into dry clothes."

Five minutes later Melissa turned into the gravel driveway and climbed the rise to the house. Maxie peered out at them from her sheltered spot under the water tank but made no move to greet them.

Melissa and Alice Ann ran through the rain to the house, Melissa noticed a curtain twitch in the cottage. Thankfully, the rain had kept Constance and the children inside. The last thing she wanted was for Alice Ann to discover them. If the girl knew people were hiding in the cottage, sooner or later she'd be bound to blurt it out to her dad. And Melissa really didn't want to ask her to keep quiet. It was bad enough that Melissa had to lie to him; she didn't want Alice Ann to do so, as well, for Melissa's sake.

"Do you want me to read you a book?" she asked after the two of them had changed and towel-dried their hair.

Alice Ann ran to her bookshelf and searched through a row of colorful volumes. "Read *Olivia?* She's my favorite."

As Melissa took the book, her eye was caught by a framed photograph on top of the low bookshelf. Alice Ann at about age two was curled up on the lap of a woman in a navy business suit who was smiling down at her. She looked as if she'd just come home from work, put down her briefcase and picked up the toddler. "Is this your mother?"

What had gone wrong between her and Gregory? Melissa had already gotten the impression that theirs hadn't been a loving relationship.

Alice Ann touched the cheek of the woman in the photo. "She's gone."

"Gone?" Surely Alice Ann didn't think her mother was at a resort, too.

"To heaven," she explained. "She drownded when I was little."

And now she was so much older.

With a sudden lump in her throat, Melissa gathered the tiny girl in her arms. "Let's start the book." She chuckled at the cute drawing of a long-eared pig on the cover and then noticed the title. "*Dream Big.* That sounds good to me."

They made themselves a cozy nest in the corduroy beanbag chair wedged between the bookshelf and Alice Ann's bed. With the rain pattering comfortably on the roof, Melissa read aloud. When Melissa was finished, she said, "With inspiration like this, a pig could do anything she wanted, couldn't she?"

Alice Ann giggled. "Olivia's clever. And funny." The little girl snuggled closer and rested a hand on her arm. "Like *you.*"

Melissa kissed the top of Alice Ann's head. She

might not know much about kids, but she knew this child was special. Clearing her throat, she continued reading.

A half hour later, Melissa looked up from the book and listened. Except for the magpies warbling in the pine trees, the world was silent. "The rain has stopped. Shall we go outside?"

They were getting on their boots when they heard Gregory's car come up the driveway.

"Daddy's home!" Alice Ann clumped across the veranda to greet him.

From the doorway, Melissa watched him swing her into his arms, the fitful sunlight making his black hair gleam. When he glanced up, the memory of their kiss was in his eyes.

The air felt charged as if after a thunderstorm. Melissa didn't know what to say. "It stopped raining."

Gregory walked to the house. "It's too late to tackle the cottage, but I thought I'd fix the fence. Would you mind giving me a hand?"

She stepped aside as he came through the front door. "I don't know anything about fencing, but I'd be glad to help."

"I need you to keep the pigs away from the broken area while I work," he explained, setting his daughter down. "I'll go change."

Melissa went toward the rear of the house and found Alice Ann coming out of the pantry, stuffing chocolate cookies in her shorts pockets. "You'll spoil your dinner," she said. "Why don't you eat an apple instead?"

"They're not for me," the four-year-old assured her. "They're for Benny."

"Oh, that's all right then," Melissa said dryly.

The rain had turned the paddocks into a sea of mud. Gregory gathered tools and supplies from the barn: a hammer, staples and a roll of mesh fencing wire. Together they walked across the yard to the paddock containing the five-month-old weaners, who were spread out down the hill all the way to the dam. The pigs were thrusting their strong snouts into the rain-softened turf, looking for worms and insects.

Alice Ann climbed nimbly over the fence, calling, "Here pig, pig, pig, pig!" Instantly, Benny trotted toward her.

The rest of the weaners, hearing the commotion, started up the hill. Melissa followed Gregory as he slipped through the gate and walked over to where the fence was broken. She squelched through the mud after him, ever aware of the boar in the next paddock watching them from the top of his mound of dirt. The horrible memory of her uncle's boar charging her flooded back, a thousand pounds of pig flesh....

With a shudder, Melissa turned away from the boar to the weaners, which were much cuter. Alice Ann was luring Benny off with cookies, but grunting and squealing, the ten other pigs made a beeline for Melissa, ears flapping. They surrounded her, sniffing her legs with their moist, wriggly noses as if to see whether she was good to eat. They must have thought she was, because the next second she felt a nibble at one rubber boot, then another at her calf. One pig got his jaws around her knee.

"They're eating me!" she shrieked. A bubble of laughter escaped her.

Chuckling, Gregory pulled a pair of wire cutters from his pocket and began clipping the section of broken mesh away from the fence post. "Pigs do have a sweet tooth."

Melissa huffed at him. How dare he calmly go about his business while she was being devoured?

Fortunately for her the weaners decided she wasn't edible and, grunting with curiosity, trotted over to see what Gregory was doing.

"Use that pig board and get them away from here," he told her, nudging a nosy weaner out of the way with his knee.

"Pig board, what's a pig board?" Melissa muttered, looking around for something that might fit that description. Propped against the fence near the gate was a rectangular piece of wood with a hand hole cut in one of the long sides.

She picked it up and flapped it at the pigs. "Shoo!"

Barking in alarm, the weaners scattered, spattering mud. Five headed down the hill to the pond, three ran to the feed trough near the gate, one jumped into the water trough. The last, a young female, wriggled through the hole in the fence right past Gregory, who had his hands full of staples and wire. Right into the boar's paddock.

Gregory swore. "Quick," he said to Melissa. "Climb over and bring her back. I'll stay here and keep the rest out."

The boar raised his head and grunted. Evil-looking yellow tusks protruded from either side of his massive jaw.

Melissa's throat went dry. "The boar's in there."

"Exactly. I don't want him servicing the weaner."

"But...but—"

"Hurry, before the other pigs come back."

Melissa glanced around for Alice Ann, but the girl was busy with Benny in the far corner of the paddock, oblivious to the excitement with the boar. Besides, it would be cowardly of her to send Alice Ann in there. Squaring her shoulders, Melissa threw the pig board over the fence into the boar's paddock and climbed after it. The animal gave another grunt and slithered down the muddy slope to level ground. Its enormous body was covered in mud where it had been wallowing.

"Here pig, pig, pig," she called softly to the weaner. One eye on the boar, Melissa circled around the young female and tapped the board on the ground to try to scare her back toward the hole in the fence.

Gregory stopped cutting and put his hands on

his hips. "Use the board to push the pig in this direction."

"Push? Oh." Melissa crowded up behind the weaner but the animal was happily rooting around in the churned up mud and grass, in no hurry to leave. "Back to the other paddock, little piggy. Come on, there's a good pig."

A low grunt from behind made her glance over her shoulder. The boar was advancing toward her. His pace picked up to a slow trot, his ponderous bulk quivering with every step.

Melissa shoved the weaner. "Move!"

With a squeal, the young pig shot forward.

Not quickly enough.

CHAPTER NINE

THE BOAR TROTTED FASTER, emitting deep earthy grunts. *Help!* She was caught between a nubile young weaner and a lust-crazed old boar.

Melissa ran after the young pig, blocking her zigzagging path with the board and funneling her toward the hole in the fence. The boar was gaining ground, his grunts coming faster and louder. When Melissa glanced back at him, his huge ears were flapping and his tusks gleamed in the sunlight. She could practically feel his loathsome breath on the back of her neck.

Only a few yards to go...

The weaner shot through the gap in the wire. Gregory closed it and quickly stapled the edge to the fence post. Melissa hurtled over the wire mesh, caught her foot on the top and fell facefirst into the mud.

The boar came to a shuddering halt, his quivering sides steaming. He lowered his head, sniffing at her through the fence. His breath came in rancid gusts.

"Are you all right?" Gregory was trying not to

laugh, without much success. "Don't be afraid. He likes you."

"I'm *not* afraid." Melissa struggled to her knees. Gregory laughed harder. "Oh, so you think it's funny to see someone wallow like a pig?"

She snaked an arm out, grabbed his boot and yanked with all her might. Gregory's eyes widened as he toppled flat on his back in the squishy mud.

"You're right!" she crowed, "it *is* pretty funny."

Gregory struggled to get up and she pounced, pushing him back into the mud. Through his shirt she could feel hard muscles, warm skin and a heart that was beating furiously.

"You like to play rough, do you?" He flipped her over and pinned her beneath him. His hands, wet with mud, slipped on her bare arms, but he managed to hang on as she struggled against his superior strength. A gleam of triumph lit his eyes as he grinned down at her.

"Hey!" She'd meant to yell, but it came out as a sigh. Suddenly she was aware of his thumbs brushing the sides of her breasts, of his hips straddling hers, and of herself spread-eagled beneath him. Then she had no breath at all.

Gregory loomed over her, silhouetted against the blue sky. His expression changed. Slowly he lowered his head. Melissa lifted her mouth, lips slightly parted, to meet his kiss....

A moist snout touched her cheek, sniffed at her

ear and began munching her hair. She screamed. "Let me up!"

Grinning again, Gregory rolled off her. Using him for support, she pulled herself to a standing position.

The weaner gazed up at her and grunted.

"Returning the favor, were you?" Melissa said dryly. Then she looked at Gregory and had to chuckle. "You're covered in mud."

"And you think you came out unscathed?" he asked, brushing clods of muck off his shirtsleeves. Then he eyed her curiously. "You *were* scared of that boar."

"No, I wasn't." She'd tried for nonchalant and was annoyed to hear the unsteadiness of her voice. Damn, they'd so nearly had a second kiss. She ought to be grateful to the weaner, but all she felt was frustrated.

"You were," he insisted. "I thought you were familiar with pigs from when you were a child on your uncle's farm?"

"When I was little my cousin Albert threw my Barbie doll into a pen with the boar. He had horrible yellow tusks and nasty piggy eyes." She crossed her arms over her chest. "The boar wasn't too handsome, either."

"What happened?" Gregory asked, smiling.

"I don't want to talk about it."

"Tell me or I'll pin you down in the mud again."

She eyed him speculatively. "You wouldn't dare."

One corner of his mouth curved. "Don't tempt me."

He was joking, but Melissa was seized by the desire to goad him and provoke him until he grabbed her and wrestled her to the earth, holding her down with his body—

Stop it! She glanced at the cottage for a reminder of why she was here. And then there was Alice Ann. The girl was still trailing around after Benny.

"I'm waiting," Gregory said.

"The boar started eating my doll." Even now, she shivered at the memory. "It was Dr. Barbie, my favorite. I climbed in to rescue her and the boar charged me."

"Boars don't charge for no reason." Gregory pulled a handful of fencing staples out of his pocket and finished hammering the new panel of wire mesh onto the fence post.

"That one did, just now!" Melissa exclaimed, pointing an accusing finger at the boar, who appeared to have gone to sleep standing up.

"Hold this," Gregory said, getting her to straighten the roll of mesh away from where he was hammering. "Boris wasn't *charging* you. He was coming over to see what was going on. The only time these animals can be dangerous is if two boars were to fight over females. Even then they're only trouble if you get in their way."

"My uncle's boar destroyed my Barbie," Melissa said. "Broke her in two and ate her upper half."

Gregory scrutinized her through narrowed eyes. "What did you do to the boar?"

"What makes you think I did anything?" Melissa blustered. Gregory arched one eyebrow. "Oh, all right. I may have stabbed him with Barbie's stiletto. I thought he was going to eat *me* next." She lifted her chin. "Anyway, he deserved it."

Smiling and shaking his head, Gregory gently wiped a smear of drying mud from beneath her eye with his thumb. "Like some humans I know, pigs are charming creatures once you get to know them."

Warmth heated her belly and her cheeks. To hell with runaways and kids and gentlemen and pigs. Planting her hands on his shoulders she leaned in—

"Melissa!" Alice Ann called as she ran over from the far side of the paddock. "Benny's collar broke. Can you fix it?" Then she stopped short and stared. "You're all muddy!"

Melissa dropped her hands and rocked back on her heels. Gregory shot her a look that spoke volumes about missed opportunities.

"We slipped and fell." Melissa winked at him, then turned and slogged off through the mud. "What's wrong with Benny's collar?"

GREGORY STRIPPED OFF HIS muddy clothes in the laundry room and put them in the sink along with Melissa's to soak. From the kitchen came the homey sounds of her getting dinner ready—the creak of the oven door as she checked on the casserole, the metallic clink of cutlery, the splash of water running into a pot. As she worked she sang a Gershwin melody in her sweet husky voice. He smiled. She was slightly out of tune and the words weren't quite right. What she lacked in accuracy she made up for in enthusiasm.

Charming creature.

She'd looked absurd and adorable flat on her back in the mud, laughing up at him. He'd wanted to rip off all their clothes and make love to her right then and there.

Yeah, right. With a dozen pigs crowding around, nibbling their bare toes.

Melissa was a mystery. She was chaotic and whimsical. Yet somehow she managed to keep the house spotlessly clean, entertain Alice Ann all day and cook a magnificent evening meal, all before he got home from work. There had to be some catch. But whatever it was, he didn't want to know. It wasn't only his daughter who'd fallen under her spell.

"Dinner's ready," Melissa called just as he came through the door, a towel wrapped around his waist. With a cheeky grin she looked him up and down.

Gregory adjusted his towel. "I'll have a quick shower and be right back."

A cold shower.

He came out of his room fifteen minutes later in a beige polo shirt and black chinos. His wet hair was slicked back from his forehead and he scraped a grain of mud from beneath his fingernail. Delicious aromas drew him to the kitchen. The chiming of the doorbell stopped him, and he went to open the door. "James!"

James Chalmers, his law professor and mentor, was on the doorstep, dressed in a navy pin-striped suit, as if he'd just come from the county court. Gregory clasped the older man by the hand, wondering at the dark circles under his eyes. "What brings you to Tipperary Springs?"

"Diane and the children, of course."

A dish crashed in the kitchen.

Gregory stepped back so he could enter. "Is everything all right?

The judge frowned. "Haven't you seen the news?"

"Not lately," Gregory replied. "I've been too busy to even read the newspaper."

"Diane, Josh and Callie are missing. They've been gone since Saturday."

"Missing!" Gregory repeated over the sound of crockery being scraped together. "That's four days."

Melissa appeared in the doorway, her face pale. She looked from Gregory to James. "Hello."

"Melissa, this is James Chalmers, a colleague of mine." Gregory turned back to him. "We were just about to have dinner. Will you stay? We have enough, don't we, Melissa?"

"Certainly," she said, unsmiling and oddly subdued.

They went into the kitchen. Alice Ann was already in her chair, to Gregory's left. Melissa set another place at the table for James, then took her own seat. She'd gone very quiet, Gregory noticed. Maybe she thought it wasn't her place to take part in the conversation. If so he would have to reassure her that she was one of the family.

"Melissa is Alice Ann's new nanny," he explained James as they sat at the table. "She's a wonderful cook."

Melissa blushed and looked down, clearly uncomfortable with the praise.

"She's modest, too." He passed the platter of chicken cacciatore and linguini to their guest. "I don't understand. What's this about Diane? Where could she have gone?"

"If I knew, I wouldn't be sitting here now." James's voice was tightly controlled. Gregory could only imagine how terrible he must be feeling.

"I don't know what to say. I can't believe this." Gregory turned to Melissa. "Did you know? Have you heard reports of a missing woman and two children in the area?"

She placed a forkful of chicken and pasta onto Alice Ann's plate. "I...I saw something on the news. Saturday evening, I think it was."

Gregory thought back as he helped himself to more pasta. "I didn't watch the news all weekend. I *did* hear a radio report about some missing persons while driving to work Monday morning, but I must have missed the names. What do you think happened? Could they have been abducted? Do the police have any clues?"

"The police are searching the Tipperary Springs area," James said. "I'm fairly certain Diane and the children aren't hurt." A blood vessel in his temple began to throb. "I haven't told anyone else this, but the truth is, she left me."

"How could that be?" Gregory asked, shocked. "You two have the perfect marriage. A big home, beautiful children. How old are the kids now?"

"Joshua is eight and Callista is six." James focused on cutting his linguini into tiny pieces. "I thought our marriage was good. Like any couple, we have the odd argument, but nothing so very bad."

Across the table, Melissa choked on her food. Coughing, she reached for her glass of water.

"Are you all right?" Gregory asked.

"I'm...fine." She dragged in a breath and released it, then took a sip of water. "The chicken must have gone down the wrong way."

"It's excellent cacciatore," James said politely. He piled the chopped linguini carefully on his fork, then added chicken. About to raise it to his lips, his mouth twisted. "It's just like Diane used to make."

Gregory glanced at Melissa, expecting her to say something comforting, but she had gone pale. Frowning, he said, "You must be desperately worried."

"You have no idea." James clenched his knife and fork. "Ever since Callista was born, Diane's had emotional problems. Depression. Paranoia. She dropped most of her friends, thinking they were all against her. At times she even thought *I* wanted to harm her."

Gregory shook his head. "Is she receiving treatment?"

"That's why I'm so concerned," the judge replied. "She left without her medication. I'm worried not only about her, but also whether she'll take care of Joshua and Callista properly. She's apt to do something…I hate to use the word but, well, crazy."

Melissa stood abruptly. Her mouth opened but nothing came out.

Gregory glanced up at her in surprise.

"I—does anyone want bread with dinner?" she asked.

"Not me," Gregory said. "James?"

"No, thank you."

"Are you feeling okay?" Gregory said to Melissa. "You look pale. You've been working too hard. Why don't you go lie down? I'll take care of everything tonight."

"No, no, I'm fine." She sat down again. "Don't mind me. Please, go on with your conversation."

Gregory studied her for another few seconds, but when she smiled gamely, he turned back to James. "You say the police are searching Tipperary Springs. Is there any reason to think she's in the area?"

James pushed away his plate, even though he hadn't finished. "The police received a tip from a man who thought he'd seen her walking along Balderdash Road. She used to be friendly with the woman who lives next door to you—Constance Derwent. I came out tonight to ask Constance if she'd heard from Diane, but she's not home."

"Constance is away on holiday," Gregory said. "I'm taking care of her chickens while she's gone."

James shook his head. "That explains why she hasn't been answering her phone. As I was leaving Constance's house I recalled that you live on Balderdash Road and realized you were her neighbor. You haven't heard anything, or even possibly seen Diane?"

"No, sorry," Gregory said. "Mind you, I've been so snowed under between work and taking care of the pigs, I haven't paid much attention to what's going on in the community. Now that Melissa's here I haven't even been to Constance's to collect the eggs." He turned to her. "Have you seen anything unusual next door?"

Eyes wide, she shook her head.

"My wife may have run to Constance, found she wasn't home and then left again," James speculated. "The question is, where would she have gone?"

"The police should be able to trace her through her credit-card transactions," Gregory suggested.

"Ah, well." James cleared his throat. "Her credit card has recently…expired."

"Expired or been canceled?" Melissa asked. When Gregory frowned at her, she met his gaze with a blank stare.

Why was she being so hostile? Couldn't she see that James was utterly destroyed by his wife's abduction of his children? Melissa was acting as though it was somehow his fault.

"Maybe Diane will return when Constance gets back," James said. "How long is she going to be away?"

"Until Sunday," Gregory told him.

"That's five days from now!" Melissa exclaimed. "Where is she?"

"She's on an outback cattle drive for tourists with her cousin from Wisconsin." Gregory had forgotten for a moment that Melissa didn't actually know Constance. So why should she care when the woman came home? Of course, she'd taken on collecting the eggs and feeding the chickens. Just another chore. He needed to lighten her workload, maybe not ask her to help him out in the yard. It wasn't that he needed her so much as he found himself looking for excuses to spend time with her.

Melissa stood and this time picked up her empty plate and gathered the others, as well. "Would you gentlemen like some coffee?"

"I'll get it. You relax." Gregory smiled at her, but she carried the dishes to the sink and left the room without returning his smile, calling to Alice Ann to get ready for bed.

"I won't stay for coffee," James said, glancing at his watch. "Thanks for dinner. Living like a bachelor these past few days has been hell."

Gregory walked him to the door. "Anytime you want to come over for a meal or just to talk, feel free."

His old friend turned on the doorstep. "Listen, Gregory, I'd appreciate it if you didn't mention to the police that Diane said she was leaving me. If they think it's a domestic quarrel they won't look for her as hard."

Gregory frowned at the floor rather than face him. "I can't lie to them."

"I'm not asking you to," James said. "Just don't volunteer the information. Who knows? Something terrible may well have happened. She could have been picked up by some nut or had an accident. I need to find her, and the police have the resources to track her down."

"I suppose…" Gregory didn't see how he could refuse.

"Daddy." Alice Ann appeared in her pajamas, holding a plastic pig from her barnyard set. Melissa stood behind her, waiting. "I've come to say good-night."

Gregory gave the child a hug. "I'll tuck you into bed in a minute." He turned back to James. "I heard you were nominated for a seat on the Supreme

Court. Congratulations, even though I'm sure that's the last thing on your mind."

"Thanks," he said. "Diane's disappearance couldn't have come at a worse time. If you see or hear anything about her or the kids…"

"I'll let you know immediately," Gregory promised. "It's hard to hide people or keep secrets in a small town. If she's here, we'll find her."

"The police will be searching all the properties in the area," James said. "In the meantime, I'll feel better knowing I can count on you to be my eyes and ears in Tipperary Springs."

"You can count on me, too." Alice Ann held the pig aloft. "Me and Detective Pig will find them!"

Gregory chuckled. He looked from her to Melissa, as he did so often lately to share his amusement. His smile faded.

Melissa had walked away. The last thing he saw was a wisp of her skirt as she turned the corner to the bedrooms.

MELISSA FLED TO HER ROOM, leaving Gregory to see James to his car. Outside her bedroom window, she could hear their footsteps crunch on the gravel and their voices, low and indistinct. Tugging the curtains shut, she switched on the bedside lamp, which cast a soft glow over the colorful quilt and pale carpet. Her thoughts were spinning in circles as she paced between the foot of her bed and the dresser. Distractedly, she noted that the irises had wilted and the dandelions were drooping, their stems dangling above the water level.

Constance wasn't returning for a whole week! At least now Melissa knew. But the police were going to search the farm. Where would Diane and the kids hide? That is, if they had sufficient warning to get out of the cottage?

And then James turning up! Melissa had almost had a heart attack. There was Gregory, giving the judge sympathy and offers of help, and not knowing what his friend was really like.

James claimed Diane was mentally unstable.

Doubt crept into Melissa's thoughts. Running away with no money and no credit cards *was* a little nuts. So was hiding in an old cottage with no plumbing and no electricity. And not going to a hospital when her son might need stitches. Okay, Diane was a nurse and probably knew better than Melissa, but still. Maybe James was right and Diane needed help. And what about Josh and Callie?

Melissa stopped pacing. *Diane* was right. James came across as completely rational and credible in the role of concerned husband. Gregory had believed him without question. Melissa might have almost believed him herself if she hadn't seen the bruising on Callie's forehead.

Diane wasn't crazy. Self-preservation was about as sane as you could get.

A knock at the door set her heart pounding. "Yes?"

"It's Gregory. May I speak to you?"

She was about to tell him she wasn't feeling well, then thought better of it. Look how easily he'd worked out that she didn't really know Constance. Pinching color into her cheeks, she smoothed her skirt, fluffed up her hair and opened the door. "Is anything wrong?"

"You tell me." His voice was gentle— deceptively so?—but his eyebrows were pulled together in a deep frown.

Melissa swallowed. "I, uh…"

"You're unwell, aren't you? Is there anything I can do?"

Oh, God! Face-to-face with Gregory, all she could think of was how kind he was and how guilty she felt lying to him. He was too sharp to fool and too honest to deceive. She was caught and didn't know which way to turn.

"I'm fine, honestly." She tried to smile convincingly.

"You don't look fine."

"Thanks a lot," she said, attempting a joke.

"You're acting strangely, too."

"In what way?" She forced herself not to twist her hands together, but keep them loose at her sides. But they persisted in clutching the folds of her skirt.

"You barely spoke a word all through dinner. I

realize you don't know James, but I would have thought that you'd have more sympathy for a man whose wife and child were missing."

"Oh, that," she said flatly, turning away.

"That's what I mean," Gregory said, following her into the room. "Sarcasm toward a man who's utterly distraught."

"Distraught?" She spun back around. "I've never seen a man *less* upset by the idea that his wife had left him, let alone might possibly be in danger. Or cold or hungry, with no one to turn to."

"He's a man," Gregory said impatiently. "Just because he doesn't show his feelings openly doesn't mean he doesn't have any."

"Then how do you know he cares about her?" Melissa tossed back. "I think he's *angry* she ran away. I think he wants her back because he needs to keep up the pretense of a stable home life. A scandal involving a runaway wife won't help him in his bid for the Supreme Court."

"Where do you get these ideas?" Gregory said. "I've known James for years. He treats Diane like a queen."

"He *would* in public." Melissa bit her lip. She was making a mistake talking like this, but she couldn't help herself. "How do you know what he treats her like in private? What if he abuses her?"

"I can't believe that."

"Why not?" Melissa threw her hands up. "You must have seen this kind of thing before in your law practice. I'm surprised you'd pass judgment without even hearing her side of the story."

Gregory leaned on the doorjamb, frowning slightly. "This sounds personal for you."

Melissa twisted her silver bangles. Had he seen through her *again?* "What do you mean?"

"Have you..." he hesitated "...been in an abusive relationship?"

"No!" She took a deep breath, relaxed her shoulders. "I have no firsthand knowledge, thank goodness. But I know that sometimes women have good reason for escaping their husbands."

"Well, sure, but this is James Chalmers. He's highly respected in the community," Gregory argued. "If there were any hint of spousal abuse it would have been known."

"If James was so good to his wife, why did she run away from him?" Melissa demanded.

"You heard him. She's been depressed, under psychiatric care. She needs help."

"I'm sure she does," Melissa said. "But again, you're taking his word against hers." Diane was right, though, Melissa thought with a creeping chill. Many people would think the same as Gregory.

"You're forgetting that a doctor would have given her a thorough medical examination," Gregory said. "She wouldn't have been prescribed medication for nothing."

"Well, why *wouldn't* she be depressed if her husband was abusing her and her children?"

"That is pure supposition on your part. It's a dangerous and potentially libelous accusation." His eyebrows made a sharper angle as his gaze narrowed. "A man's reputation is at stake. If he's discredited he could lose custody of his children."

Melissa was struck by Gregory's fervor. "It's personal with *you*."

He glanced away, a muscle in his jaw twitching. "I have never abused anyone, nor have I ever been accused of such a thing."

"That's not what I meant. Did you have a custody battle over Alice Ann?"

"We're not discussing me."

"We are now," Melissa said. "What happened?"

"It's none of your business," he said roughly.

"No," she admitted. "But...I care."

He stared at her, and Melissa's heart seemed to stop. Then it beat hard and fast. Gregory clenched his jaw. Was he deciding whether or not he could confide in her? Or was he wondering just how big a problem it was that she was falling for him?

"I have to tuck in Alice Ann," he said at last. "Good night."

"Good night," Melissa replied, more disappointed than she liked to think.

He paused at the door. "I meant to tell you earlier and forgot when James arrived...the butcher is coming tomorrow afternoon for the weaners."

"Have you told her yet?"

Gregory shook his head. "I don't want to do it just before bedtime. I'll talk to her when I get home tomorrow afternoon before the butcher arrives. Then I'd like you to take her somewhere so she doesn't see the pigs being loaded and taken away."

"Don't worry, she'll forget about Benny when Ruthie's babies are born."

The lines around his mouth deepened. "I hope you're right."

CHAPTER TEN

ALICE ANN CLIMBED on a stool to look in the pantry. Only two cookies left. She took one for herself and one for Benny, then searched for something else he would like. A muesli bar, dried figs, half a bar of cooking chocolate, a few marshmallows that had fallen out of the bag and gotten lost behind the canned vegetables… She crammed everything into the pockets of her purple jeans until they were bulging.

"Alice Ann," her father called. She could hear his footsteps in the hall as he came looking for her. "Where are you? I want to talk to you."

Uh-oh. He was going to make her pick up her toys. And he would make her put the goodies for Benny back. She waited until she heard him go into the lounge room, then ran out the back door onto the veranda.

A truck was coming up the driveway. Good. Daddy would have to talk to the driver. Alice Ann darted across the yard to Benny's pen. "Here, pig, pig, pig."

All the piggies came running, but she could pick out Benny easily with his shorter pink stripe. With his pretty blue collar it was even easier. Daddy said he was only a runt, but she thought Benny was the smartest, and he could run as fast as any of the others.

Benny stopped in front of her and wiggled his nose in the air, sniffing to see what she'd brought him. Alice Ann giggled. "You've got a big nose."

Reaching into her pocket, she pulled out the cookie. Ignoring the other pigs that crowded around, she fed it to Benny. It was only fair. He was always last to get his snout in at the feed trough.

As she peeled the wrapper off the muesli bar she glanced over at the truck. It was white and dirty and had a wire fence around the open back, like a tiny pigpen. It stopped in front of the barn and a man got out. He had a greeny-brown shirt and greeny-brown pants and a hat with a wide brim. Her daddy came out of the house and shook the man's hand. She could tell they were talking about the pigs because Daddy was pointing to the pen where the weaners lived. He waved at her to come up to the house but at that moment Benny nudged her leg and reminded her he was still hungry.

"Do you want a muesli bar?" she crooned, backing up a step as she held out half of it. Daddy wouldn't let her put a lead on his collar, so she was teaching Benny to follow her.

He trailed after her around the feed trough and

along the fence. She wished she could take him out of the pen and around the yard, but Daddy always said no.

"You wouldn't run away or get into the grain like Ruthie did that time, would you, Benny?"

The animal grunted.

"That's right. You would stick close by me and be a good little piggy wiggy."

Alice Ann fed Benny the half muesli bar and scratched his ears. He flopped onto the ground and lay on his side so she could scratch his belly. Alice Ann laughed. Benny looked as if he had a big smile on his face.

The man got back in his truck. Instead of driving away he backed it up to the gate of the weaners' pen.

"Alice Ann," Daddy called, walking over. "Go up to the house. Melissa's going to take you to the library."

She shook her head. She was being very naughty, but she really didn't feel like going to the library. Books were good, but the library lady was always shushing her.

"You need to go now," Daddy insisted.

Then the driver said something through his window and her daddy shook his head because he was annoyed with her and started walking to the machine shed.

The man got out of the truck and went around to lower the back flap. He nodded at Alice Ann. "G'day."

She stepped over to the fence. "What are you doing?"

The man unhooked the bolt on the gate and came into the paddock. "Soon as your dad gets here with the ramp I'm going to load up them pigs."

"And take them to the pig resort?" Alice Ann asked eagerly.

"Pig resort?" He burst out laughing. "That's a good one."

"Daddy said the weaners are going to a resort," she insisted. "There are beautiful green paddocks and a special pig chef."

Still chuckling, the man took his crumpled hat off and scratched his neck. "These pigs aren't going to no resort. They're going to the abattoir to be made into pork chops."

Alice Ann felt cold all over. "Pork chops? You mean, you're going to *kill* them?"

The man slapped his hat back on his head. "The bloke at the abattoir slaughters 'em. I butcher 'em. Once they've been gutted and skinned, I carve them up into chops, roasts and hams and sell them in my shop."

Alice Ann stared at him, horrified. No fresh green paddocks, no lovely gourmet pig slop. "*Benny's* not going to the aba...aba..." she stammered at the unfamiliar word.

"Abattoir," the man repeated. "Is Benny that runt nibbling at your pants?"

She nodded.

"He ain't no good for anything else."

"He is, too!" she shouted. "He's my friend."

Startled, Benny woofed in surprise and darted away.

"Where do you think your breakfast bacon comes from?" the man asked. "Little pigs like that one."

"You're a bad man!" Alice Ann turned and called Benny. She had to protect him. "Come back, Benny."

The pig stopped beside the empty feed trough and looked at her from beneath his floppy ears. Then she saw her daddy walking toward them with the metal ramp under his arm.

"Daddy," she called, clambering over the gate to get to him. Tears flooded her eyes and she couldn't see. She tripped and fell as she jumped off the gate, hurting her knees. "That bad man said the weaners were going to the aba...aba...to be killed!"

Her father dropped the ramp and crouched to gather her into his arms. "Shh, sweetheart. Don't cry."

Alice Ann buried her face in his shirt and breathed in his familiar scent. She could feel her heart pounding really fast and she felt so small compared to the man and the truck. But her daddy's arms were around her, keeping her safe. He would keep Benny safe, too.

"Benny won't be made into a pork chop, *will* he?" she begged, her voice muffled by his chest.

"Now, Alice Ann." His voice sounded sad, like when he'd told her that Mummy had had an accident and wasn't ever coming home. "I wish I *could* tell you that. The truth is, Benny is going to the abattoir, too."

"No!" she shouted, pushing away from him. "You said he was going to a pig resort. I won't let you take him away!"

"We'll talk about this later."

"No!" She climbed back over the gate into the paddock with Benny.

Frowning, he started toward her. *"Alice Ann."*

The man with the truck said, "I don't have all day, mate. Let's load these pigs."

"Alice Ann, go up to the house," her father said, using his stern voice. "Melissa's taking you out." Then he picked up the ramp and started for the paddock.

Alice Ann crouched beside Benny and hugged him around his thick neck. He made grunting noises and snuffled against her pocket, where he could smell the figs. "I won't let them take you, Benny, I promise."

She would run away from home and take him with her. They could join the circus Melissa had told her about. Circus people would love a smart pig like Benny. Alice Ann would wear a pink sparkly bathing suit and pink feathers on her head. Benny would have pink feathers on his head, too, and jump through flaming hoops. Everybody would clap and cheer.

Feeling better, she wiped the tears out of her eyes and peered over Benny's back. They had the ramp propped against the back of the truck and her dad was pushing the weaners up it with the pig board. Now was her chance to save Benny, but she had to hurry.

Alice Ann ran over to the gate and slid back the steel bolt, keeping an eye on her father to make sure he didn't see her. Then she pushed the gate open just wide enough for her and Benny to get through.

"Here pig, pig, pig," she called quietly. She held out a dried fig.

Benny trotted over, grunting.

"Shh," she cautioned as she retreated, leading him through the gate. Her heart was beating really fast and she felt sort of excited and sort of scared, like the time she'd gone too fast on the merry-go-round at the park. Then her father looked over and saw her, and she thought she might be sick.

"What are you doing?" he yelled. "Get that pig back in the paddock!"

She hesitated, but only for a second. Then she turned and ran. "Come on, Benny!"

She heard another shout and glanced over her shoulder. The pigs on the ramp had gotten scared when her daddy shouted. They woofed and tried to run away, falling off the ramp onto the ground. *Then* they ran, some into the barnyard, some across the open field behind the farm building toward the woods, some squealing down the driveway toward the road.

Her father said a bad word. The man with the truck said lots of bad words. Maxie started barking. Both men shouted and chased after the pigs.

Alice Ann didn't wait to see any more. She turned and ran, too, slipping between the barn and the cottage. She would hide in the bush behind their farm. She would find a hollow tree and live there like a possum until she could figure out how to get to the circus—

She stopped short, and stood—blinking. A girl was coming out of the old outhouse. Alice Ann stared at her. The girl wore a yellow top and blue skirt and her reddish blond hair was in pigtails. She stopped, too, and stared back.

"Who are you?" Benny nibbled at Alice Ann's legs. Absent-mindedly, she fed him a fig.

"I'm not supposed to tell anyone." The girl hopped from flagstone to flagstone on the path between the outhouse and the cottage, then stopped halfway.

"Daddy says not to go in there," Alice Ann said, nodding at the outhouse. "'Cuz of redback spiders."

"I had to. I was busting." The girl glanced toward the cottage. She licked her lips.

Alice Ann looked in that direction, too. Her eyes widened. The back door to the cottage was open a crack. "I'm not allowed to go in *there,* either. My daddy says it's dangerous."

"Don't tell anyone," the girl begged.

"I won't," Alice Ann replied. "Me and Benny are running away from home. We're going to join the circus."

"You're too little to join the circus," the girl said scornfully.

"Am not!"

"And they don't have pigs in the circus."

"They do, too!" Alice Ann forced away the pinpricks of tears and stuck out her chin. "Come on, Benny." She marched past the girl, wading through the long grass and weeds and trying not to feel scared about snakes.

"I ran away from home, too," the other girl said.

Alice Ann slowed and turned, curious. "You did?"

She nodded, her mouth turned down. "It's not much fun."

"Well, *I'm* going to have fun," Alice Ann declared. "I'm going to live in the bush and have animals for friends. Just till I get to the circus."

"You won't have your own bed or your dolls and toys," the girl pointed out. "None of your friends will be around to play with." She bit her bottom lip and her voice wobbled. "Your daddy won't know where you are."

At that, Alice Ann almost cried. She was mad at her father, but she couldn't imagine not being with him. She needed her daddy to tuck her in bed at night. No one else knew their special good-night, not even Melissa.

"I have to save Benny," she whispered.

The sound of men's voices had been faraway. Now she could hear them coming closer. If she was going to run across the open field to the bush she had to go now. But just thinking about it made her knees feel shaky.

The girl heard the voices, too, and started chewing on the end of her pigtail. "I have to go inside now."

Even the forbidden cottage, dark with dangers only hinted at by her father, seemed better than getting lost in the bush. Who knew if she would even find a hollow tree? And Benny needed a hiding place right now. "Can Benny and I come?"

The girl shrugged and ran across the overgrown paving stones to slip inside the cottage. Alice Ann held out a marshmallow to Benny. "Here pig, pig, pig." She coaxed him inside and shut the door.

After the bright sunlight outside, Alice Ann could hardly see, but the air was cool and smelled funny. She stood very still, afraid to move in case whatever bad thing lived in the cottage came to get her.

A moment later a thin yellow beam danced along the floor. The girl had a flashlight. Alice Ann found she was in a tiny kitchen. In the other room there was a whole lot of furniture and boxes.

"Who's this?" someone said in a sharp whisper.

The light beam shone on Alice Ann's face. She

raised a hand to shield her eyes and the beam dropped to her legs.

"It's Alice Ann," the girl said.

"How do you know my name?" she asked.

The girl shone the flashlight on a woman standing in the doorway to the other room. She wore light brown pants and a white top.

"We hear your father calling you," the woman said. "You'd better go back before he comes looking for you."

"I'm never going back."

"She's running away from home," the girl explained. "I told her she shouldn't."

Benny grunted and his hooves made a clicking sound on the slate floor. The woman let out a squeal like Benny did when he was getting fed. "What is a pig doing in here?"

"Can we keep him?" the other girl asked. "He needs to be saved."

"We can't keep a pig. We have enough trouble staying hidden as it is." The woman crouched down in front of Alice Ann so she could look her in the eye. "Why are you running away from home, darling?"

"Because of Benny," Alice Ann said, feeling somewhat better because the woman seemed kind. "I'm hiding him so he won't get made into pork chops."

"I *like* pork chops." Up from the couch popped a boy's ruffled head.

"You can't have Benny," Alice Ann said, alarmed at his sudden appearance. How many people were living in here?

"He won't hurt your pig." The woman rose. "But I'm afraid you can't hide him in here. This is a cottage not a stable."

"Pigs don't poo in their houses," Alice Ann said earnestly. "They're very clean."

"That may be so but—"

"Please, Mum!" the girl begged. "He could sleep with me."

"Don't be stupid," the boy said. "We could put him in the laundry room," he added to his mum. "It'd be fun to have a pig for a pet."

"Pigs make noise, which would attract attention," the woman said firmly. "Plus, he'd have to go out sooner or later. Someone would see him and come to investigate."

"Please don't make me take him back." Alice Ann heard her voice quiver, and put a hand on Benny so she would be brave and not cry.

The woman edged around the furniture to the window and peered out a crack in the curtains. "Your father and the other man have mustered those pigs and are loading them onto the truck."

"Why are you living in our cottage?" Alice Ann asked. "Why don't you turn on the lights?"

"We have no place else to go right now," the woman said. "We have no light because the electricity isn't on. Besides, we don't want anyone to know we're here. We're waiting for the woman next door to get home."

"The egg lady?" Alice Ann asked. "She's nice."

"She's a friend of mine. Until she gets back we need to stay hidden."

"I won't tell," Alice Ann said. "If you hide Benny."

"Alice Ann!" her father called. "Where are you?"

"You'd better go," the woman said.

"What about Benny?"

"We can't keep him inside all day and night."

"I'll take him out while my daddy's at work."

"Alice Ann!" Her father was closer.

"Okay," the woman agreed quickly. "We'll keep Benny in the laundry room if you go right now. Run around the other side of the barn so your father doesn't know you've come from the cottage."

"Okay." Alice Ann turned to her pig. "Did you hear that, Benny? You're going to be saved."

"Quick now." The woman opened the back door and peeked outside. "It's clear. Remember, run all the way around the barn. If we're safe, Benny will be safe."

Alice Ann slipped out the door, dashed across the narrow gap between the cottage and the barn, then ran along the back and came out between the barn and the house.

"Where have you been?" Her father strode toward her. His face was flushed red from chasing pigs and his eyebrows were pushed together. "What have you done with Benny?"

"I—" Alice Ann's voice got stuck. She couldn't tell him about the people in the cottage or Benny wouldn't be safe. Anyway, she didn't know their names. So she said the first thing that came to her. "*My friend* saved him."

"I have no time for your games," he snapped. "There are no other girls for miles around. Who the blazes are you talking about?"

Alice Ann twirled her fingers through her hair, tangling them in the long dark strands. "My friend."

"What friend? Where does she live?"

She shrugged. She knew where the woman and her children were staying; she didn't know where they *lived.*

His nose flared. "How old is this girl? It *is* a girl?"

She nodded, her fingers going around and around in her hair. "Older than me."

"Don't do that." Gregory puller her hand away from her head. "Older than Amber?"

Amber was her eight-year-old cousin. "Don't know."

"Oh, for crying out loud." Her father glanced back to the truck.

The other man had finished loading the pigs. Ten weaners milled in the back. Some pushed their snouts through the wire mesh, sniffing the air. With a screech of metal on metal the man slid the bolt through, fastening the flap to the frame of the truck.

"You go in the house," her father said to her. "We'll discuss this later."

Alice Ann nodded and ran off. She might get into trouble, but that was okay. The only thing that mattered was that Benny was safe.

"ALICE ANN, it's important that you tell me the truth." Gregory pulled up his daughter's light coverlet and shifted his weight on the bed. "Did you see which direction Benny ran off in? Did he go across the field and into the bush?"

Alice Ann began to twine her fingers in her hair. "He's with my friend. And I *am* telling the truth."

Not this again. Gregory tried another tack. "Maybe the thought of Benny being killed is so upsetting that you made up someone who could save him?"

At this reminder of the abattoir, Alice Ann's face clouded. "You lied to me. You said Benny was going to a pig resort."

The reproach in his daughter's eyes was almost unbearable. His heart heavy, Gregory tried to explain. "I didn't want to upset you. I should have made it clear that on a farm, the main reason we raise the pigs is for the meat. You like bacon and pork roasts, don't you?"

She nodded, eyes shiny with unshed tears.

"To eat meat we have to kill the pigs," he went on, trying to be matter-of-fact about it. Taking her small hand, he held it gently. "That's why I don't want you to make pets out of them or to name them. It makes it that much more difficult when we send them to the abattoir."

"We named Ruthie."

"It's different with the breeding sows. They'll be with us for many years." He decided he might as well get everything over at once. "Eventually Ruthie, too, will have to be slaughtered—when she gets old."

A single tear rolled down Alice Ann's cheek. He wiped it away with the pad of his thumb, his heart breaking just looking at her. "Some things in life aren't very nice, are they?"

She shook her head and drew in a deep, shuddering breath that racked her small chest.

"But you know, sweetheart, for the time that Ruthie and Benny are with us they have a good life. They live in a paddock and run around in the sunshine. They eat grass and dig for worms and insects, which is how pigs are supposed to live. We don't inject them with hormones or chemicals and make them live in cages. They have as natural a life as we can give them."

"Ruthie's finished making her nest," Alice Ann said, sniffing.

"Has she? There, you see? She's happy because she can have her babies out in the open on the soft grass."

Alice Ann gave him a wan smile. "When will the babies come?"

"They'll probably arrive in a few days." He paused, listening to Melissa's footsteps on the veranda through the open window. She often went out for a walk in the evening while he had his quiet time with Alice Ann before bed. An image of the nanny formed in his mind—the soft shine of moonlight on her bare shoulders, the tinkle of her bangles. Her smile, seductive and mysterious.

Gregory turned his attention back to his daughter. "When Ruthie's babies come, I don't want you to get attached to them, not even if there's a runt."

"I won't," Alice Ann said. "Benny will still be my favorite."

Gregory winced. Had anything he said made an impression? "It's time to go to sleep. Benny will probably turn up tomorrow.

He switched off the light and went quietly out of the room. Melissa's door was ajar, and as he went past he could see she hadn't come in yet. He didn't feel good about their disagreement over James last night, and they hadn't had an opportunity to talk again.

Gregory pushed open the screen door and went outside in search of her.

CHAPTER ELEVEN

MELISSA HAD HALF EXPECTED Gregory to seek her out, so she'd cut her visit to Diane short. She heard the creak of the screen door when she was halfway across the barnyard. To cover up her real purpose, she stopped by Ruthie's nest and leaned on the fence to gaze at the sleeping black hump. Beyond was the sloping hill and the moonlit pond.

Her heart was beating fast as Gregory moved with a loose-limbed grace toward her in the moonlight. The long shadow slanting from his heels across the yard emphasized his height. His eyebrows stood out black against the pewter planes of his strong face.

He came to a halt beside her at the fence, his arm brushing hers. She shivered, her awareness heightened in the intimacy of the night.

"How's Ruthie? No babies yet, I see."

"Um, no." Melissa's guilty secret gnawed at her, all the more so because it had just gotten bigger. The cottage's population had grown by one small pig. "Is Alice Ann still upset about the weaners going to the abattoir?"

"Not as much as I had expected. She doesn't accept that it will happen to Benny." He turned to Melissa and a lock of dark hair fell over his forehead. "She has an imaginary friend who 'saved' him."

"An imaginary friend?" Melissa relaxed a fraction. Alice Ann hadn't given Diane and the children away. But the thing she hadn't wanted to happen, had. The little girl had been drawn in to keeping a secret from her father. If Gregory found out and knew Melissa was involved...

"She's so desperate she really seems to believe another girl has materialized to save Benny. I can't help but worry about her. I mean, where does she think that pig is?"

"It's natural for you to worry—you're her father." Melissa touched his arm, intending merely to comfort. Her hand lingered a moment too long. He must have felt so, too, for he held her gaze; his dark and unreadable. With another shiver, she withdrew her hand, "There are worse things than an imaginary friend, a lot worse," Melissa said. "Lack of food and shelter, lack of love. Abuse."

Gregory sighed. "I suppose I do need to keep things in perspective. But the longer Alice Ann holds on to the idea that an imaginary friend can save her pig, the more difficult she'll find it to accept the truth about Benny's fate."

Oh, God. Now Melissa was contributing to Alice Ann's problems. If only she could tell Gregory the truth and ease some of his worries over the child. But she couldn't do that without exposing Diane. The lies and secrets kept compounding with every day that passed. Diane hadn't told Alice Ann that Melissa was helping them for fear of compromising Melissa's position on the farm. And Melissa couldn't explain the situation to Alice Ann because that would force the girl to be party to an even bigger lie to her father. Luckily, Alice Ann had accepted Diane and her children's presence without question, as long as Benny was safe. Oh, what a tangled web we weave...

Melissa pleated the soft folds of her skirt and tried to think what she would be saying right now if she didn't know where the little pig was. "If Benny's lost we don't actually know what his fate will be. Could he survive on his own in the woods?"

"Easily," Gregory said. "There are feral pigs all through this area, lost from farms over the years." He scratched the back of his head. "I just can't figure out why Alice Ann isn't more upset at losing Benny. I'd have thought she would be begging me to look for him."

"She's four years old. She lives in the moment. She probably hasn't given a thought to when or if Benny will reappear as long as he wasn't on the truck going to the abattoir.

Gregory gave Melissa a puzzled smile. "How is it you know so much about kids?"

"I empathize, I suppose." She turned her head

away. "When you love someone you don't want to lose them."

He tucked a long strand of hair behind her ear, exposing her face to his gaze. "Is that how you felt about your acrobat?"

"Oh, no," she said quickly. "I liked him a lot but I don't think I really loved him. He was fun, exotic, frivolous. Everyone thought he was perfect for me and yet he…he left me craving *substance*."

Gregory tilted his head quizzically as if he would have liked her to expand on this statement.

Instead, she changed the subject. "I'll have a talk with Alice Ann tomorrow. We'll take a walk up to the woods to look for Benny."

"Thanks." Gregory squeezed her shoulder, his hand lingering a moment on her bare skin.

"It's late," Melissa said reluctantly. "I guess we'd better go in." Once inside, they would go to their separate rooms as they did every evening, he to do paperwork, she to read.

"Not yet." Gregory folded her chilled fingers between his warm palms. "It bothers me that we fell out over James and his wife. I wish I could convey to you how much I look up to him, professionally and personally. He was one of my law professors years ago and he helped me a great deal when I was a student. He wrote me a glowing reference for my first job. His own career has been stellar."

"I don't know James," Melissa replied. "But I do

know that marriages aren't always what they seem on the surface."

"That's true," Gregory conceded. "But the few times I was at their home, James was attentive and complimentary to Diane, drawing everyone's attention to her beauty, publicly commenting on her fine dinner. Diane seemed very happy. I can't believe James would hurt her."

Melissa ached to tell him everything, but she couldn't say a word without betraying her inside knowledge. Oh, if only it all wasn't so complicated.

"Can you just trust me on this?" Gregory asked.

"I would trust you with my life," she said simply. "James is lucky to have a loyal friend like you. Time will tell about him and Diane."

Gregory's gaze dropped to their linked hands. "I haven't been able to get you out of my head all week," he said softly.

Melissa swallowed. "You haven't?"

At the tremble in her voice, his eyes flashed to hers. He reached up to cup her cheek, and she pressed her face into the warm hollow of his hand. His lips brushed her neck. "Have you thought about me?"

"I've thought about doing *this*." Holding his gaze, she slid her fingers through his dark hair. She shut her eyes in a sensual bliss. It was just as thick and silky as she'd imagined, slipping over her hand like water. Then his mouth was on hers, and he pulled her close, crushing her against his chest. She'd fallen for him so fast; could this be real? She hadn't been looking for a lover, not so soon after Julio, but Gregory was like no one she'd ever known.

He drew back, his breathing erratic, to trail his hand down her neck until his knuckles lightly caressed the curve of her breast. "I know I told you I wouldn't take advantage of our situation. I didn't count on being so attracted to you. But if we both feel the same way…"

Melissa disentangled her hand from his hair. She couldn't lead him on while she wasn't being honest. Maybe when Constance came home and Diane was out of his cottage, Melissa could tell him the truth—

There, her train of thought went off the rails. As soon as he knew she'd lied to him he would lose interest. She placed a hand on his chest. "This is happening too quickly."

"You want to slow down," he said, clearly disappointed.

Melissa's insides were churning. What she wanted was an honest relationship. Why couldn't they have met under simpler circumstances? "We don't know each other very well."

Gregory settled his hands on the curve of her hips, anchoring her to him. "Then we'll just have to remedy that."

"Don't you think it would be confusing for Alice Ann to see us being affectionate after such a short time?" Playing on his feelings for his daughter was hitting below the belt, but there were bigger issues at stake.

"You're right," he said at last. "I was letting my emotions cloud my judgment. If things didn't work out between us it would be awkward. I'm sorry. It won't happen again."

"Well, you don't have to get *too* remorseful," she said, perversely annoyed that he'd given up so quickly. "It was only one kiss."

"Oh, I don't regret kissing you," he said. "I regret that I can't make love to you."

Though he was no longer touching her, his low voice softened her like melted butter. She wished... She wished for so many things she couldn't have. He was chief among them.

Gregory lightly touched her cheek then stepped back. "You're too tempting. This weekend I'll *definitely* clean out the cottage so you can move in."

"Fantastic," she said, her heart sinking. "Cleaning out the cottage will solve all our problems."

MELISSA GLARED at the amiable-looking police sergeant and his constable standing on the bottom step of the veranda. It was Friday, two days since Benny had "disappeared." They'd hidden him from Gregory successfully so far but now a pig wasn't the only one in danger of being discovered.

"You'll have to wait until Mr. Finch returns," Melissa told the policemen. "I don't have the authority to let you search the property."

Sergeant Carmichael was lean and exceptionally tall, with black hair and green eyes. "If I have to obtain a search warrant I will, but I'd rather people cooperate."

Melissa would rather he gave up and went away but it didn't look as if she would get her wish, either. She, Diane, Josh and Callie had been out in the yard when the police car had turned in the driveway. There'd been no time for Diane and the kids to run across open fields to the woods, no time to cut through the orchard to Constance's chicken coop. Instead they'd dashed straight back into the cottage, like hunted animals going to ground. As far as Melissa knew, they were still there, trapped.

"Perhaps you could call him at work and ask," Constable Burns suggested. He was a fresh-faced young cop with a pink complexion and fine sandy hair.

Just then, Melissa heard Gregory's car in the driveway. Her heart jerked erratically. "He's home," she said bluntly. "You can ask him yourself."

The Volvo crested the top of the rise and parked next to the police car. Gregory got out. Alice Ann darted out from behind Melissa and ran down the steps. "Daddy!"

"What's going on, possum?" Gregory scooped her into his arms and carried her back to the house.

"The policemans want to go in the house and Melissa won't let them."

Gregory threw a questioning glance at Melissa. She responded with a disdainful shrug, challenging him to find fault in her defending his property. Inside, she was quaking. Disaster seemed inevitable.

"Can I help you, Sergeant?" Gregory asked.

"G'day, Mr. Finch. Constable Burns and myself are conducting a house-to-house search in the area. Ballarat police received a tip from a motorist that a missing woman, Diane Chalmers, and her children were seen on Balderdash Road last Sunday."

"So I'd heard," Gregory said. "Is there a problem?"

"Your nanny…" Sergeant Carmichael nodded at Melissa "…was reluctant to let us in without your permission."

"You're welcome to search the property," Gregory said. "I'm a personal friend of James Chalmers and I've met his wife. I'll do whatever I can to help you find her."

"Thank you," Sergeant Carmichael said. "We'll start with the house."

Melissa could do nothing except stand aside as Gregory ushered the policemen inside. She was about to follow them down the hall to the bedrooms when Gregory grabbed her hand and pulled her into the kitchen. "Could I have a word with you in private? Alice Ann, go play in the living room, please."

Oh, hell. Melissa lifted her chin. "Yes?"

"Why did you give those men a hard time about doing their job?" he said. "You should know I would agree to a search by the police. I have nothing to hide." He paused. "Do you?"

She could hear closet doors being opened and closed. Tiny drops of perspiration formed on Melissa's upper lip. "Why would you even think that?"

"I don't know." He threw up his hands. "Every time I think I'm getting to know you, that we have something special, you do something that eludes my understanding."

He really felt something for her. Melissa experienced a brief surge of elation, quickly followed by despair because his caring made her deception so much worse. "I didn't want them going through your things without you being here," she explained, and hoped it made sense to him. "*I* don't know whether you have anything to hide or not."

"As a lawyer, as a citizen, I would never do anything illegal," he said, adding dryly, "So for the record, I'm clean."

Sergeant Carmichael returned from searching the bedrooms, and Constable Burns emerged from the laundry room, shaking his head. Alice Ann wandered back to the kitchen where everyone had congregated.

"Is the motorist the only lead you've got?" Gregory asked. "It seems strange that no one else has seen her."

"She's either in hiding or has met with foul play," Sergeant Carmichael said. "No bodies have turned up yet—"

"May I remind you, Officer," Melissa interjected, "there's a small child present."

"I know what fowl play is." Alice Ann piped up. "It's what chickens do after school."

Sergeant Carmichael chuckled. "That's right." He turned to Gregory. "We'll search the outbuildings now. Do you have a key for the cottage?"

"It's not locked," Gregory said. "This is the country. Besides, if anyone wants to steal a lot of old furniture, they're welcome to it."

"If you're searching the cottage, I'll go, too," Melissa said, panicking.

Alice Ann tugged on her father's pant leg. "They shouldn't go in the cottage!"

Gregory glanced from Melissa to Alice Ann. "Why not?"

"It's…it's dangerous." Alice Ann pushed her fingers in her hair and started twirling. "You said not to go there."

Gregory told the officers, "There are piled up boxes and broken outdoor furniture stored in there. Not a place for a four-year-old to play."

Sergeant Carmichael smiled at Alice Ann. "Thanks for warning us. I think we can handle it."

Gregory held the back door open. The police

filed out first. As Melissa passed, Gregory asked, "Why are you so keen to be there?"

Without quite meeting his eyes she said lightly, "Naturally, I want to see where I'm going to live."

Gregory went ahead with the two police officers. Melissa and Alice Ann followed, clutching each other's hands. Melissa imagined the sergeant opening the bedroom closet in the cottage and finding Diane, Josh and Callie huddled inside.

"The previous owners used to rent the cottage out as a farmstay," Gregory was telling the policemen when Melissa and Alice Ann caught up to them. "Their furniture and some household items are still in here." He turned the knob and pushed the door open.

Melissa and Alice Ann surged forward, but Sergeant Carmichael thrust out an arm. "Hold up, there. If this place hasn't been used in nearly a year there should be thick dust everywhere. We don't want everyone making tracks and disturbing clues."

A darn good reason for her to get inside, Melissa thought, determined to follow him. She smiled apologetically and stepped back, biding her time.

The constable flicked the light switch by the door. Nothing happened.

"The electricity has been turned off at the mains," Gregory explained. He reached around and pulled the draw cord on the curtains.

Light flooded into the lounge room, which was

crammed with furniture. Piled on the couches were pillows and old towels, a ceramic lamp swathed in Bubble Wrap and stacks of plastic food containers. In the far corner was an assortment of large cardboard boxes.

"It's even more of a mess than I remembered," Gregory muttered. "It'll be a chore to clear this out."

The police edged through the narrow gap between the furniture and the wall. Constable Burns got down on his hands and knees and shone a flashlight under the couches and chairs, but it was obvious there wasn't room for anyone to hide there. Melissa watched, gripping her hands together. Thank goodness Diane had replaced the kitchen chairs upside down on the table. Luckily the rough slate floor didn't show footprints. Now, if only the officers didn't notice the absence of dust on the breakfast bar....

But the cops bypassed the galley kitchen and disappeared into the short hallway to the two bedrooms. Melissa let out her breath.

"If there are people hiding in my cottage, I want to be on hand to see it," Gregory declared, and stepped over the threshold.

"If you're going in, so am I," Melissa murmured, and went in after him.

"Me, too." Alice Ann took Melissa's hand.

Together they made their way through the cottage, Melissa glancing in every shadowy corner.

Her heart was pumping, shooting adrenaline through her veins so fast she felt queasy. Any moment, she expected to hear Callie cry out or Josh start sneezing.

The police were in the main bedroom. There was the queen-sized bed with its bare mattress and folded blankets at the foot. A painting of the pond and the willow tree hung over the bed. A chest of drawers with a mirror stood against the far wall.

Melissa held her breath when the constable got down and peered under the bed. She'd barely recovered before the sergeant opened the closet door and shone his light inside. He stood there so long she could *hear* her heart thumping. Finally, he turned away. "Nothing but dust bunnies and mouse droppings."

Melissa glanced at Gregory. "You'd better get a mousetrap if you expect me to move in here."

Sergeant Carmichael noticed them hovering in the doorway. "I thought I told you lot to stay outside." He frowned at the trio. "Please stay in one spot and let us do our job. Constable Burns, go check the back of the cottage."

Ignoring the sergeant's edict, Melissa followed him to the second bedroom, Alice Ann and Gregory on her heels. The door of the bedroom was slightly ajar. Melissa's palms were damp and she wiped them on her skirt. There weren't many hiding places left. Sergeant Carmichael slowly pushed the door open.

No one was in the room. Melissa's shoulders relaxed and she heard Alice Ann release a soft sigh.

The tension returned when Sergeant Carmichael began to search under the twin beds, which were also bare with blankets piled at the foot. Her mother's red-and-gray wool blankets, Melissa noted with a start. Fortunately, Gregory didn't seem familiar with the previous owners' possessions.

An old-fashioned wardrobe leaned into the room next to the window. Sergeant Carmichael put his fingers on the round brass knob of one of the doors. Melissa heard the click of the catch releasing and held her breath. The hinge creaked as the door swung slowly open. She crossed her arms over her stomach, certain she would be sick. Wire hangers dangling from the rod clanged together as the officer poked his head inside.

"What's this?" he said sharply.

Melissa, Gregory and Alice Ann crowded closer.

On the floor, crammed into the back, was a bulging black garbage bag.

Sergeant Carmichael dragged it across the floor of the wardrobe. "It's heavy," he grunted.

Melissa stomach turned over.

Beside her, Gregory muttered, "If there's a body in there…" He turned to her. "Take Alice Ann and get her outside—"

"Holy Christmas!" Sergeant Carmichael exclaimed. "Will you look at this!"

He pulled down the plastic to reveal a large

Santa Claus. Rounded on the bottom and weighted, when Sergeant Carmichael pushed, the figure rocked back and forth, emitting a wheezy holiday tune.

Melissa sank onto the bed and dropped her head between her knees. Spots swam before her eyes. Gregory's hand settled on her back, solid and comforting. "It's okay. Just a lawn decoration."

Then from the kitchen Constable Burns called, "Sarge, come quick!"

Sergeant Carmichael hurried from the room. Gregory, Melissa and Alice Ann followed. They all crowded into the alcove between the tiny kitchen and the laundry room.

Constable Burns pointed at the closed door. "Listen."

Everyone stood still. A scuffling noise came from there, followed by a breathy panting. Melissa was careful not to look at Alice Ann. She put her hand out and the little girl clung to it.

"Open the door," Sergeant Carmichael said impatiently.

Constable Burns turned the handle and pushed.

Benny rushed out, squealing and grunting. Alice Ann opened her arms, but he dodged through the forest of legs, dashed down the narrow chute between wall and furniture and through the open front door to freedom.

Alice Ann ran after him, calling, "Benny, come back."

"That solves one mystery," Gregory said, scratching the back of his head. "Though, how he got in here is another. Melissa?"

She was still struggling to catch her breath. "Beats me."

While Constable Burns shone his flashlight in the dark corners behind the furnace, Sergeant Carmichael examined the back door. "The door is shut tightly. That pig didn't get in here by accident. Someone had to have let it in."

Gregory nudged an old ice-cream container half full of water with his foot, and nodded at the pile of grass on the laundry-room floor. "I'm afraid my daughter must be the culprit, Sergeant. She's been fretting over that pig since she found out he was destined for the abattoir yesterday. She let it out of the paddock. I thought it ran into the woods, but she must have put it in here."

"The bottom line is Diane Chalmers and her children aren't here," Sergeant Carmichael said. "Let's go."

Relief turned Melissa's knees to jelly. She put a hand out to grasp the doorjamb for support, but found Gregory's shoulder instead. His arm went around her waist and she leaned into him.

"I'll check the outhouse, Sarge," Constable Burns said.

"You'd have to be truly desperate to shelter in there," Melissa protested. But it was just possible.

"It's a good place to dump a dead body," Constable Burns replied cheerfully.

"After that we'll be on our way," the sergeant said to Gregory. "I appreciate your cooperation."

They'd started to file back out of the cottage when Gregory stopped. "I think I'll lock that back door. I don't want Alice Ann bringing Benny in here again."

Melissa waited for him at the front, nervous at him being alone in the cottage. The police were no fools, but Gregory missed nothing.

His back was turned to her when she heard the sneeze. Melissa's heart stopped. *Josh.* They were here, in this room. Suddenly she realized where the Tupperware and pillows scattered on the couches had come from: the large boxes piled in the corner.

"What was that?" Gregory demanded, looking about.

"I sneezed," Melissa said quickly, and faked another. "It's the dust."

Gregory's eyes narrowed. She forced herself not to look over at the boxes. He shrugged and went to lock the back door. Then, as he passed through the kitchen on his way out, he stooped to pick up something wedged beneath the rubber mat in front of the sink. Melissa bit her lip. *What now?* But he gave it only a cursory glance before putting it in his pocket.

Constable Burns had made quick work of the outhouse. He and Sergeant Carmichael got in their squad car and drove off, dust rising as they disappeared down the driveway.

Gregory helped Alice Ann put Benny back in his paddock, while Melissa walked to the veranda and sat on the leather couch. She leaned back, her mind spinning and shut her eyes. Diane and her children were safe. Gregory hadn't noticed anything.

"Why didn't you tell me you've been in that cottage before today?"

Her eyes snapped open. Gregory was standing over her. Glancing at the nearby paddock, she saw that Alice Ann was still with Benny. "What are you talking about?"

He opened his fist to show her a hair clip.

At first she didn't understand the significance of what she was looking at. "What's that?" she asked blankly.

"You should know. It's yours. Just like the one you lost in the barnyard."

"Oh!" She snatched it out of his hand. "Thank you. I was wondering where—" She broke off, realizing she was caught, and trying to salvage the situation. "I must have lost it when we went inside."

He glanced at her hair, shaking his head. "I'd already noticed you weren't wearing hair clips today." He added quietly, "Just as I notice everything about you."

He waited.

"Okay, you caught me," she said with a heavy sigh. "Yesterday, when Benny got out and we were searching for him, I went around back of the cottage and noticed the door ajar. I looked inside and there he was. I felt sorry for Alice Ann being so upset that I…I didn't stop to think. I shut him in the laundry room and went out."

"Did she know?"

"Um…" Melissa stalled.

"I want the truth," Gregory demanded.

"She must have put Benny in there," Melissa said. "I didn't say anything because *I* didn't want to be the one responsible for her pig going to the abattoir. I was going to try to persuade her to do the right thing and give him up herself."

"You lied to me *again,*" Gregory said. "You deliberately went behind my back and acted against my express wishes. Anyone else I would fire on the spot. Why should I make an exception in your case?"

"Because I did it out of love for Alice Ann and…"

"And what?"

"Nothing. Just that. I acted out of compassion. I would do it again if I had to." She glanced away, biting her bottom lip. "I wouldn't blame you if you fired me."

Gregory paced away down the veranda, head bent, hands on his hips as he considered his verdict. Finally he came back to where she was sitting. "I believe you when you say you did it for Alice Ann," he said gruffly. "You're misguided, but your heart is in the right place. You're not fired."

"Thank you," she replied, relief flooding through her. "Will you tell Alice Ann you won't send Benny to the abattoir?"

"I can't do that. We have a new litter of pigs every couple of months. She can't get attached to every runt that comes along."

"There's been another litter since Benny's, and she hasn't made pets out of any of them," Melissa argued. "It's only him she's attached to."

"What happens when he grows up and isn't cute anymore?" Gregory countered. "She'll find another one to make into a pet."

Unable to answer, Melissa was silent.

"Now that she knows the truth, she'll get used to the idea," Gregory added. "It's the reality of life on a farm."

"She's only four years old," Melissa protested. "What does she know about reality?"

"I'm trying to teach her," Gregory said. "The sooner she learns, the better off she'll be."

"We all need a balance," Melissa said. "Maybe *you* should indulge in a little fantasy."

"What do you mean?" he asked warily.

She pictured him naked and tied to a bed while she, in a short sexy nurse's uniform, taught him about discipline. Her cheeks grew hot. "Never mind. Dumb idea."

But as she went to open the door, she suddenly turned back to give him a quick and searing kiss. "That's for my second chance."

Before he could say a word, she hurried inside.

CHAPTER TWELVE

MELISSA AWOKE EARLY the next morning and quickly pulled on her jeans and a top. She tiptoed down the hall to Gregory's closed bedroom door. Holding her breath, she listened: not a sound. He must still be asleep. On tiptoe, she went on to Alice Ann's room. The door was ajar so she peeked in. The little girl was breathing regularly, eyes closed.

Melissa quietly went out through the kitchen, taking care not to let the screen door slam, and ran down to the cottage. She gave her special knock and stepped inside the darkened lounge room. "It's me, Melissa."

Diane peered around the corner from the bedrooms. "Thank goodness!" Hurrying forward, she hugged her. "Ever since yesterday I've been expecting another visit from the police, once they realized they hadn't searched as thoroughly as they could have."

Melissa gave her an extra squeeze for the ordeal she'd been through. "I was terrified when Josh sneezed. I expected Gregory to go straight to the boxes and find you."

"*You* were scared? I thought my heart was going to stop!" Diane pressed a hand to her chest. "Thank goodness you stalled the police long enough for us to empty out three of the boxes and climb in."

Melissa laughed. "Good thing you're five foot two instead of five foot ten."

"Lucky, too, that I practice yoga. I'm amazed the police didn't notice the sides of the boxes quivering. I think it's the longest Josh has ever been still without being asleep."

Sobering, Melissa handed over Callie's other hair clip. "Gregory found this and assumed it was mine. I had to tell him I knew about Benny being in the laundry room."

"I feel terrible, putting you in this position," Diane said. "Oh, I wish Constance would come home. Is Gregory still planning to clean out the cottage today?"

"Yes, but don't worry. I'm going to invite him and Alice Ann to my sister Ally's house for my birthday. Birthday lunches in our family are always a day-long affair. In fact, I have to bring a dish to the party. Do you have any suggestions?"

"Pasta salad is pretty straightforward," Diane said. "Try a bit of honey in a creamy mustard dressing. It gives the salad a lift."

"Honey? I never would have thought of that." Melissa sat on the arm of a brown corduroy couch.

"Diane, I think it's time I told Gregory about you being here."

"Oh, no!" she exclaimed. "Constance is due back in a couple of days. Can't we just wait?"

"Listen, please," Melissa begged. "I can't keep putting him off about cleaning the cottage. Gregory's a really good man. Once he knows the whole story he wouldn't let anything bad happen to you."

Diane paced the tiny kitchen, darting worried glances at Melissa over the breakfast bar. "He's a friend of James. If you're wrong and he tells my husband where I am, bad things will happen automatically."

"We can trust Gregory," Melissa insisted. "And, well, the thing is, I want *him* to be able to trust *me*." Diane studied her with new interest and Melissa dropped her gaze.

"You're falling for him!" It wasn't an accusation but an expression of delight.

Melissa sighed. "I don't want to keep lying to him."

Diane went silent, stewing over the problem. Finally she lifted her hands. "I think it's a mistake, but okay, go ahead. I've disrupted your life enough as it is. I don't want to mess up your love life, too."

"Calling it a love life might be a touch optimistic, but I live in hope." Melissa thought for a moment. "I'll wait until tonight to tell him, though. I don't want my birthday spoiled just in case he's not as understanding as I believe he'll be."

Melissa edged her way back through the furniture to peek around the curtains. Good. No one was in the yard. She turned to Diane and gave her another quick hug. "I know you're worried about your safety with Gregory knowing. But everything will be okay. I promise."

She ran back to the house and slipped in through the back door. A moment later, Gregory came into the kitchen dressed in work pants and an old shirt.

"Good morning!" she said, reaching for a large pot from the bottom cupboard. "You're up early."

He pulled the phone book from a shelf under the counter and started looking through the Yellow Pages. "I'm going to hire someone with a truck to help me take that furniture out of the cottage. No more delays."

"Oh, but you can't." Melissa didn't even have to pretend dismay. "It's my birthday and you and Alice Ann are invited to the party at my sister's house."

Gregory tucked a finger between the pages and looked up. "You mentioned your party, but not that Alice Ann and I were invited."

"With the police here yesterday, I forgot. I'm sorry it's such short notice. I'd really like it if you could come. Ally's expecting you."

"The cottage—"

"Can it wait another day?" Constance would be

home tomorrow and everything would be fine. "Please."

"Well, okay." Gregory put the phone book away. "Thank you."

"Wonderful!" She meant it and not just because of Diane. She was looking forward to a whole day in his company without chores or conflicts of any kind.

She ran water into the pot and set it on the stove to boil. Then she gathered the ingredients for her salad—carrots, broccoli, green onions, grated cheese, mayonnaise, mustard and honey.

"This is the first time I've witnessed you cooking up one of your fabulous dishes," Gregory commented as he set up the espresso machine for lattes. "What are you making? It doesn't look like breakfast."

Melissa poured spiral pasta into the boiling water. Gregory's scrutiny was making her nervous. She ignored him and concentrated on following the recipe. It *seemed* simple enough. She'd made changes to the dressing as per Diane's suggestions, guessing at the quantities of some ingredients, but with luck it should be edible. "It's a pasta salad for lunch today."

"I'm looking forward to meeting your family," Gregory said. The aroma of fresh coffee filled the room. "Are they all as capable and efficient as you?"

Uh-oh. Too late, Melissa saw the pitfalls of her

little scheme. Her family all thought of her as a hopeless, if lovable, ditz, and treated her as such. "I've got to warn you, my dad is kind of eccentric."

"Eccentric," Gregory repeated. "In what way?"

Melissa began to chop the vegetables. "Tony's... well, he's *Tony*. If he starts asking you about legal loopholes, run, don't walk, in the other direction."

"Ah, a businessman." Over the hiss of steaming milk, Gregory asked, "And your mother?"

Melissa threw him a blurry glance over the chopped onions. "Mother would like me to settle down. She might get embarrassing, you being an eligible bachelor."

Gregory placed a frothy, fragrant latte beside the chopping board. "As long as she doesn't have a priest in attendance."

"If she does, he'll be giving her last rites after I'm through with her," Melissa said darkly.

"What about your sister?" Gregory asked. "Is there anything I should know about her?"

"Ally obsesses about everything being in its proper place. She'll have name cards for the seating arrangement, you can bank on it. But she's loosened up a lot since she and Ben got married." Melissa dumped the drained pasta in a big, stainless steel bowl. "She's great, though, and so are my parents. I don't know why I'm telling you all this."

"You want me to like them," he said. "That's natural."

Melissa sipped the coffee, savoring the creamy, bitter flavor. She'd never cared if Julio had liked her family. Maybe because she'd never seriously believed their affair would last. Not that she and Gregory were even having an affair, much less something lasting. "They'll like *you,* I know that."

Gregory stared at her with a steady gaze until she felt heat tinge her cheeks. Then *he* seemed to grow uncomfortable. Setting his latte aside barely touched, he moved toward the back door. "If we're not going for a while I'll start pulling some of the smaller stuff out of the cottage."

"Wait!" she cried, racking her brains for some way to stall him. He paused, eyebrows raised. Seizing the honey jar, Melissa stuck a finger in and pulled out a big glob of the sweet stuff. "Taste this. I got it at the market. It's homemade by a man in Bulla."

Slowly, Gregory walked over to where she stood with honey oozing down her finger. He took her fingertip in his mouth. The moist, sucking warmth sent a sexual charge straight through her. Melissa heard a buzzing in her ears as if bees were swarming in the kitchen. Heat tingled through her blood in the steamy kitchen.

He let her hand go and lowered his lips to hers, drawing in her tongue in place of her finger. She tasted honey, fragrant with gum flowers, and rich dark arabica coffee. And the most seductive flavor of all: Gregory. Helpless to resist, she wound her arms around his neck and rose on her toes to deepen the kiss. God, she was terrible. Yesterday she'd pushed him away in an attempt to be honorable. Today she was using sex to manipulate him into staying out of the cottage. But to be honest, right this minute, she didn't give a damn what excuse she used.

At last he drew back, his breathing irregular. He smoothed a strand of hair off her cheek. "Honey with pasta?"

"Just a dash in the dressing," she replied, swallowing when she saw the dark gleam in his eyes. "Gives the salad a lift."

He brushed a kiss over her lips and across her cheek. "I'm not so sure I want you to move into the cottage."

Melissa placed her palm on his chest just to feel his heart beating. "I'm not in any hurry to go."

"Daddy! Melissa!" Small footsteps pounded down the hallway. Gregory and Melissa moved apart. Alice Ann stopped short in the doorway. "What are you guys doing?"

"Cooking," Melissa said quickly.

"We're going to Melissa's birthday party later," Gregory told his daughter. "After breakfast you and I need to take a trip into town."

"To buy her a present?"

"I was trying to be subtle, but yes." Gregory exchanged a smile with Melissa.

"A birthday party!" Alice Ann danced around the room. "Yay!"

GREGORY HELD the back door of his Volvo open. A four-year-old princess in her best satin dress and her hair done in ringlets, climbed in. Alice Ann was thrilled to be invited to a grown-up birthday party. "Melissa's my favorite nanny ever, Daddy," she whispered. "She's going to love our present."

"I hope so." He helped his daughter find the seat buckle among the folds of purple fabric. Then he placed the wrapped gift beside her. "You haven't given her any hints, have you?"

Alice Ann put a finger up to her mouth and solemnly shook her head. "Not a peep."

"Good girl." Then he was distracted by Melissa coming out of the house. She wore a flowing ivory skirt and sleeveless coffee-colored lace top with a plunging neckline that set off her creamy skin and striking red hair. From her ears dangled the white beaded-and-feathered earrings she'd had on the first day she'd come up the lane in her Beetle. She looked magnificent. And sexy as hell.

"You look great." She cast an admiring glance at his crisp, tieless white shirt and sports jacket.

"You took the words right out of my mouth." He breathed in her floral scent as she slid past him and into the passenger seat.

Ally and Ben's house was a white weatherboard cottage high on Wombat Hill. Gregory parked on the street out front because the driveway was taken up by a blue utility truck and a black Audi convertible. Fragrant jasmine wafted on a breeze from the flowering vine growing along the side fence. They went through a white-painted iron gate and up a couple of steps onto a veranda. The front door stood open.

Melissa knocked and walked in. "Hello! We're here."

Gregory glanced around. To his right was the lounge room, comfortable and appealing, painted in a bold saffron with colorful accessories and interesting artwork.

Melissa saw him admiring a painting. "The watercolors are Ally's. They're terrific, don't you think?"

He'd barely murmured agreement before Ally herself rushed out of the kitchen, her shoulder-length brown hair flying. A cloisonné butterfly was pinned to her fuchsia cardigan. "Come in! We're in the back garden." She offered her hand to Gregory. "Hi, I'm Ally."

An elegant woman of about fifty followed Ally into the room. She wore a black sheath dress with silver accessories and her blond hair was twisted into a chignon. "I'm Cheryl, Melissa's mother," she said, extending a well-manicured hand. "Delighted to meet you."

Gregory murmured greetings and introduced Alice Ann, who was cooed over with great enthusiasm by the ladies.

"How are your friends' renovations going?"

Cheryl asked Melissa. "Am I going to get my blankets back anytime soon?"

"Oh!" Melissa started guiltily. She glanced at Gregory. "I don't believe they've got the heat going yet. Do you need the blankets particularly?"

"No," Cheryl said. "I was just wondering." She continued to gaze at Melissa as if expecting some further information.

"I, um, haven't seen them since last weekend," she added weakly. "I'll call."

"I must be working you too hard if you don't have time to visit your friends," Gregory said. "You should take tomorrow off."

Melissa shook her head nervously. "No, that's okay."

"Come outside," Ally urged. "The table's set up under the pergola. We're about to play a game of croquet."

The table was laden with cheeses and rustic breads, olives, salamis and fresh tomatoes chopped up with garlic and basil. Bottles of wine gleamed in the sunlight filtering through the leaves of the bougainvillea entwined in the pergola. The delicious aroma of roasting lamb came from the barbecue. On the lawn, which was brown after a long dry summer, two men were pushing hoops into the ground, while a towheaded boy whacked wooden balls with a mallet.

Alice Ann ran over, clearly having forgotten she was wearing her best princess gown in her eagerness to play. The younger man, who had spiky blond hair, glanced up with an easy smile. "Who wants a game? We'll have to play teams."

"Let's mix it up," Ally suggested. "I'll play with Melissa, Ben and Mother can be a team, and Tony and Gregory. Alice Ann can be partners with Danny."

Melissa introduced Gregory to Ally's husband, Ben, and their father. Then she said, "I'm not sure this arrangement is going to work."

"Don't worry," Gregory said, removing his jacket and turning up his sleeves. "We'll go easy on you."

"*We* won't go easy on *you*," Cheryl said, linking arms with Ben. "Will we?"

"We'll demolish all opposition," Ben said cheerfully.

"Here, Alice Ann." Danny handed the little girl a wooden mallet with yellow stripes. "I'll teach you to how to knock our opponents' balls off the pitch."

Alice Ann took a practice swing at a yellow ball. "Like that?" she asked, as the ball rolled into the bushes.

"No," Danny replied patiently. "*Other* people's balls."

Tony pounded the last stake in the ground and straightened, pushing a hand against his lower back. He wore a beret, an open-necked shirt and a pair of very baggy trousers.

"I like the French look." Melissa adjusted the angle on her father's dark blue hat. "When did you change your persona again?"

"I never change, *chérie,* I merely reveal another facet of my complex personality," Tony replied with dignity. "This week I put my first vintage into French oak barrels. It's a robust Shiraz, which promises to be of exceptional character."

Gregory looked on, amused and charmed. Seeing Melissa with her family was as revealing as Tony's costumes apparently were. She wasn't just an efficient housekeeper and a caring nanny. She had her mother's sense of style, her sister's infectious laughter, her father's extravagant personality and her own unique blend of impudence and vulnerability.

The game proceeded with great hilarity and copious amounts of wine. Gregory laughed along with the others at Melissa's clowning around. Despite having seen evidence of her lighthearted nature at the farm, he was nevertheless amazed at how frivolous she became with her family. The affection in their good-natured teasing left him in no doubt that Melissa was a favorite.

"You're a different person today," he commented to her as they sat down to lunch under the shady pergola.

"How so?" Ally said, passing him a bowl of salad. "She's the same as always. Ditzy and disorganized—"

"Hey!" Melissa complained.

"I mean that in the nicest possible way," her sister assured her with genuine affection.

"Around the farm she's a model of organization," Gregory told them. "She keeps the house immaculate, cooks gourmet meals and still finds time to play with Alice Ann."

"Immaculate?" Cheryl repeated in disbelief.

"Gourmet meals?" Ally queried, eyebrows raised.

Tony stabbed a forkful of roasted eggplant in Melissa's direction. "You've found your niche—housewife."

Melissa choked on a sip of Shiraz.

"Darling," Cheryl protested, "she's going to have a career."

Gregory reached for Melissa's pasta salad, which sat untouched in the center of the table. "I can't wait to try this." He turned to Ben. "I understand you taught her everything she knows about cooking."

Ben barked out a laugh. "Melissa, I love you like a sister. But don't blame whatever this is on me!"

"They do enjoy teasing you, don't they?" Gregory said. He scooped out a large spoonful of pasta salad and passed the bowl to Ally. "Try it. You'll see what a great cook she is."

Tony raised his glass. "It must be love."

Melissa moaned. "This is so embarrassing."

His mouth watering in anticipation, Gregory took a bite. A moment later his smile faded at the unpleasantly sweet taste. Okay, so she'd been heavy-handed with the honey; he'd been distracting her. He chewed doggedly. The half-cooked pasta had the consistency of an old tire. Suddenly conscious that everyone was watching him, he smiled even though he felt like gagging. Finally he managed to swallow. "Delicious."

"He's very polite," Cheryl commented to Melissa approvingly.

"Poor Mel," Ally said. "You've got to give her credit for trying."

"I know it's awful, okay?" she countered.

"It's not so bad." Gregory discreetly pushed the pasta salad to one side of his plate.

He passed her the platter of roast lamb, which Ben had sliced into mouth-watering chunks dressed with rosemary, garlic and roasted lemon. Melissa took a piece and added it to the salad and the roast potato on her plate.

"Aren't you feeling well?" he asked solicitously.

She smiled up at him. "I'm fine."

"What's wrong?" Cheryl inquired from across the table. "Is Melissa sick?"

"That's what I wondered," Gregory replied. "Normally she has a…hearty appetite."

"*Normally* the girl lives on tea and toast because she can't be bothered to cook." Cheryl raised her glass of chardonnay to Ben. "Fabulous as always."

Gregory frowned, recalling the midnight snacking and the way leftovers disappeared during the day. Then Tony started telling a story about his olive harvest, which segued into anecdotes from Ben's restaurant. After the meal, Ben brought out Melissa's birthday cake and Ally piled presents in her sister's lap.

She received clothes, books and perfume, all thoughtful and insightful gifts from people who knew Melissa's tastes. Gregory exchanged a glance with Alice Ann as his daughter passed her their present. He hoped she would like it.

"What can it be? Give me a hint," Melissa teased as she ripped the wrapping off the large square box. Alice Ann giggled but said nothing. Melissa undid the flap, burrowed through tissue paper and pulled out a blown-glass pig with huge floppy ears. Instead of black and pink, the glass shimmered in iridescent blues, purples and greens, with flecks of gold leaf pressed into the surface.

"We went to a glass artist, gave him a photo of Ruthie in her slimmer days and watched him make it," Gregory explained.

"He had a fire right in his *house*," Alice Ann said.

"A kiln in his studio," Gregory translated, taking Alice Ann on his lap. "He rolled the ball of glass on a long metal tube—"

"And he huffed and he puffed and he blew it up like a balloon." Alice Ann added gestures to illustrate. "Then he made ears and legs and a curly tail."

"It's the most beautiful thing I've ever seen."

Melissa turned the translucent pig this way and that to catch the light. "Thank you so much."

The sun was a red streak over the distant purple hills when they finally stood on the front lawn in the cooling evening air to say good-night. The tail-lights of Cheryl's Audi were receding down the road. Although it was past Alice Ann's bedtime, she was wide-awake and chattered about the party all the way home. Once there, Gregory read her a short storybook, tucked her into bed, then went in search of Melissa. He found her on the back veranda. She was leaning on a post, gazing out over the sloping paddocks, where the pigs were black humps in the gray grass.

"I enjoyed your family," he said, standing beside her. "Did you have a good time?"

"Yes." She seemed pensive.

Gregory brushed her hair back so he could see her profile. "Were they too hard on you? Teasing isn't always funny."

"They weren't teasing. You see, I've been pretending to be someone I'm not." She sighed and turned her troubled blue eyes in his direction. "I'm a hopeless ditz. I always have been and I always will be."

"You're not. You're funny and smart and capable. Capable of anything you put your mind to as long as you believe in yourself."

"I can't really cook. It's a sham."

"Anyone can have an off day."

"I *can* clean."

"I know you can." He pulled her into his arms. "You're fantastic and I'm crazy about you."

"Gregory, there's something I have to tell you—"

"I'm not going to listen to another word against you," he said, kissing her eyelids. She relaxed in his arms and he felt a surge of power that aroused all his protective instincts.

"But it's important," she protested.

"So is this," he murmured, and kissed her.

CHAPTER THIRTEEN

MELISSA SLIPPED HER ARMS around Gregory's neck and felt his encircle her waist. As their bodies touched, her resolution to tell him the truth wavered.

But guilt nagged at her. "Gregory, I want—"

"Me, as much as I want you?" He ran his hands down her back, then pressed her hips to his.

"Mmm, I can tell that's quite a lot," she murmured, moving against him. "And I do want you, but…we…need to…talk about the cottage."

"Not the cottage," Gregory groaned. He scattered kisses across her cheek and jaw, nuzzled her neck.

Melissa shivered as his lips set her nerve endings tingling. "Do you seduce all of Alice Ann's nannies?"

"She's just had three, including you. You're the only one I've even kissed."

"If the other two look like Mrs. Blundstone, I'm not surprised."

"Actually, they were quite attractive." His fingers slipped lower to caress her breast.

"I don't want to hear about them."

"I don't want to talk about them." He kissed her again. "I'm interested in *you*." Dark hair fell across his forehead, giving him the look of an intellectual pirate.

He picked her up, and with a giddy rush, she tightened her hold around his neck. Nudging open the back door, he carried her inside, through the kitchen and into the hall. Her dangling foot set the hall table wobbling, while her shoulder knocked a painting on the opposite wall. She reached out to straighten it but they were already past, heading swiftly for his bedroom.

"Gregory!" she exclaimed, laughing.

"Shh, you'll wake Alice Ann."

"Just try not to bruise me!"

"Don't worry. I'll be gentle with you."

Her heart slammed against her ribs. Beneath her palm his chest was a solid wall of muscle. She strained upward to kiss him. "Please don't. Be too gentle, that is."

Gregory turned her in his arms and she wrapped her legs around his waist. She felt the rough scrape of denim on her inner thighs and the cold metal of his belt buckle through her lace panties. With his breath harsh in her ear, they bumped through his bedroom door and he closed it behind them. Then he was laying her on his bed, and she was sinking into the chocolate-and-cream linen of the pillows and comforter, her skirt pushed up around her thighs.

Straightening, he unbuttoned his shirt, the methodical action at odds with his burning gaze. He flung his shirt away, and Melissa took in his broad, muscled chest with its smattering of dark hair across the golden, rippling skin. Had she really thought him too old for her?

Melissa's gaze dropped lower, following the narrow line of hair that ran down his abdomen and disappeared below the waistband of his jeans. Jeans he was now unzipping.

Naked, he pulled her back to her feet and drew her blouse over her head. He traced the curve of trembling flesh above her bra. "You're beautiful."

She'd wanted so badly to feel his hands on her body. She'd thought about it night after night. Now she was in his bedroom and it was all happening.

Gregory undid the catch on her bra, releasing her breasts into his hands. His mouth, hot and moist, closed around a hardened nipple. Melissa's blood quickened, suffusing her with heat until her body felt swollen and lush. She undid the catch on her waistband and her skirt slipped away in a silken whisper.

Together they fell onto the bed in a tangle of limbs, rolling over until she was on her back and Gregory was trailing kisses down her body. His lips brushed her inner thighs, making her skin ripple. He pulled off her panties and she lay naked before him. The cool air from the open window caressed her hot moist skin, and she shivered deliciously.

"You are *so* beautiful," he whispered.

Melissa raised her arms and pulled him down to her. The sensual shock of skin on skin stole her breath. She dimly remembered her intention of telling him about Diane. Then Gregory moved against her, shifting her legs wider as he settled deeper, and all thoughts fled. He pressed against the entrance to her soft slick passage. Her swollen tissues throbbed with every tiny movement he made.

"Are you waiting for an invitation?" she asked huskily.

With exquisite tenderness that didn't mask the strain his powerful body was under, he kissed first one corner of her mouth, then the other. "Yes."

Inexplicably, tears filled her eyes. "Make love to me," she whispered. "Please."

"That would be my greatest pleasure."

And it was, for both of them.

ATOM BY ATOM, consciousness came to Gregory. First he was aware of light and shade, then form and shape, followed by a slow focus on details. The glow of the bedside lamp left on after they'd fallen asleep, the shadows in the corners of the room, the digital clock reading 4:00 a.m. Smooth legs entwined with his.

His face was buried in a fragrant mass of hair.

He noticed crumpled sheets. The sweaty slickness of skin. The earthy scent of sex.

He and Melissa had made love, fallen asleep, then woken up and made love again. The heady realization rocked him. Nothing would be the same from now on. She wouldn't move into the cottage. For a while they would have to be discreet. Gradually they could tell Alice Ann what was going on…

Melissa's eyes opened, pools of midnight blue. "Hey, there," she said with a dreamy smile.

"Hey, yourself." He rolled off her and pulled her with him so they were lying on their sides, face-to-face. "Last night was so good. I haven't felt that way since…" He trailed off as she snuggled closer, all her soft curves molding to his hard angles, making his body flare to life.

"Since when?" she asked lazily.

He stroked down her back, tracing the curve of her hips. "I can't remember. Never."

She eased back, searching his face. "Since Alice Ann's mother?"

At the mention of *her,* Gregory rolled onto his back. "I never loved Debra."

"Do you want to tell me about it?" Melissa asked softly.

"It's not a happy story." He hadn't spoken to anyone in several years about how Alice Ann was conceived and it wasn't easy to relive the painful memories. He turned onto his side so he could look at Melissa. Her eyes were warm with understanding before he even said a word. If he and Melissa were to have a future, she ought to know his past.

"Debra wanted a baby and unbeknownst to me, she decided I would make a good sperm donor," he began, unable to keep the bitterness from his voice. "Problem was, she never told me. She kept up the relationship just long enough to get pregnant. After that she severed all ties. Or tried to."

"That's awful," Melissa responded, rising on her elbows. "Who was she? How did you know her?"

"She was a partner in the law firm I worked for in Melbourne," Gregory said. "She'd recently turned forty and was feeling her clock ticking down. I figured that out afterward. One night after work she bought me a drink in the bar and, well, seduced me."

Frowning, Melissa subsided onto her pillow. "I saw her photo in Alice Ann's room. She *looks* nice, but, obviously, appearances can be deceiving."

Gregory smoothed the furrows from Melissa's forehead with his thumb. Her outrage on his behalf eased some of his own, which still burned even after four years. "She was very attractive and she could be charming. I certainly liked her for a while. She adored Alice Ann and was a good mother. Except for one thing…she didn't want a man in her life, or to share Alice Ann."

"It wasn't right for her to get pregnant without your consent, but it takes two to tango," Melissa pointed out. "If you didn't want a baby, why didn't you take precautions?"

"In hindsight, I *should* have." Gregory bunched the sheet in his fist, recalling how unfair Debra's actions had been, not just to him, but to Alice Ann. "She told me she was on the pill. She assured me the sex was safe."

"Ah. Then you had every right to be angry." Melissa began to massage his forearm, her fingers working to soften the knotted muscles.

"I'll never forget the day I found out she was pregnant. She was still at the law firm, although we hadn't been together in weeks. I thought she'd just put on weight until one of the other partners asked her when her baby was due." His breath failed him even now. "It was like a punch to the gut."

"Suddenly you were a father when you weren't ready." Melissa's voice was full of sympathy.

"Alice Ann was never the problem," he said earnestly. "From the moment she was born I was hooked on that kid. Even before that I wanted her."

Melissa laid a cool palm against his cheek. "Debra should have considered herself lucky to find a man who cared so much for her child."

"Debra claimed she didn't know who the father was. She refused DNA testing."

"You only have to look at Alice Ann to know she's your daughter."

"Even when she was a few months old, that was evident," Gregory agreed. "She has my eyebrows, my widow's peak." He pushed up his hair to reveal the sharp dip in his hairline. "I've since had a DNA test done and found out that Alice Ann is my biological daughter."

"It must have been awful to be denied your own child," Melissa said softly.

"Terrible." His voice thickened as he remembered the helpless rage. "Debra wouldn't allow me to even see Alice Ann. She wouldn't accept child support. She got the best family lawyer in Melbourne to fight for what she insisted were her rights. Alice Ann was *her* baby. No one else's. It became very ugly."

Melissa stroked up his arm, across his shoulder and down his chest, as if by soothing him, she could erase his anger and pain. "What did you do?" How did you get custody of Alice Ann?"

"I fought Debra in court. I wanted joint custody, or at the very least, access." He paused. "Then one day she was out on the bay in a sailboat. It was one of those freak accidents. A storm blew up, she got hit on the head by the swinging boom and was swept overboard. She wasn't wearing a life jacket. Before anyone could throw her a lifeline or jump in to save her, she drowned."

"Oh, my God," Melissa said. "How awful."

"It was dreadful for Alice Ann. I've been trying to make it up to her ever since."

Melissa squeezed his hand. "I'm sorry she lost her mother. And I'm sorry Debra put you through such hell. You didn't deserve it. You're a good father."

Gregory shrugged. "I try. It's not always easy."

"You need to be kinder to yourself." Melissa traced a fingertip around his mouth. "Learn to enjoy life more."

He captured her finger and took it in his mouth, recalling the taste of honey on her skin. "You could reform me, lighten me up. You might make it your life's work."

She tilted her head as if considering the matter judiciously. "I *am* looking for a challenge."

Outside, a pig started grunting in a low staccato burst of guttural noise. Gregory heard it and ignored it, leaning in to kiss Melissa.

The pig's grunting became interspersed with harsh panting.

Melissa pushed Gregory away and propped herself up on her elbow, her head turned toward the window. "What *is* that?"

"Relax, it's just Ruthie having her babies."

"Shouldn't we go out there?" Melissa threw back the covers. "She sounds as if she needs help."

Gregory smiled and pulled her back under the doona. "She's fine on her own. Animals work on instinct."

"Don't you need to call the vet?"

"No. She can take care of it. In the morning we'll go see the piglets." He smoothed Melissa's hair off her forehead. He felt better having told her about

Debra. It was almost as if she'd shared his trials over Alice Ann and they were in this together. Then he remembered—she'd wanted to tell him something. "What was it you were so anxious to say to me last night?"

A pucker formed between her eyebrows. "Oh, yes. *That*. Well…" She eased away, creating more space between them. "I know how you set great store by honesty."

"Now you know why." Gregory captured her hand and raised it to kiss her knuckles one by one. "To tell you the truth, I felt so burned by Debra that I swore off women. I had trouble trusting anyone. Until *you* came along."

Melissa swallowed. "Oh, God."

A high-pitched squeal rent the quiet night. She shot to a sitting position. "You can't tell me *that's* not a pig in trouble."

"Sometimes the piglets have trouble finding their way to a teat," Gregory said, frowning. "But they'll sort it out on their own."

"Are you *sure* you shouldn't call the vet?"

"I'm positive. I've been through this before with one of my other sows. Plus all the breeders have told me the same thing."

Even so, he listened with a growing sense of unease as the squealing continued and Ruthie's grunting became more agitated. Ruthie was a first-time mother, after all.

The squealing intensified to a high-pitched

scream, then abruptly stopped. Relaxing, Gregory tucked a lock of hair behind Melissa's ear. "You were saying?"

Melissa flashed a smile, but she still looked anxious. "Do you remember the day I first came up your lane—"

"Shh!" He held up a hand, listening. He'd heard another sound besides the noise the pigs were making. There it was again. A knock at the back door.

"Who the hell could be knocking at this hour of the night?" Gregory got out of bed and threw on his robe. "Wait here."

He left Melissa sitting up in bed, clutching the covers to her chest.

When he opened the kitchen door, a young girl's face peered through the screen. "Who are you?"

"I'm Callie," the girl said. "Mum said to call you because there's something wrong with your pig. We heard the noises and—"

"*Callie,*" Gregory interrupted. He opened the screen door for a better look. "You're not... Are you...Callista *Chalmers?*"

"Um, yes." The girl twisted her hands together. "One of the piglets got squashed."

"What are you doing in my barnyard?" Even as he asked, the pieces slotted into place. Melissa's sudden appearance the very day Diane Chalmers and her children disappeared. Her lies about

Constance. The pantry bulging with groceries. Melissa's midnight excursions and Benny finding his way into the shut-up cottage. Even the hair clips Melissa had claimed were hers were this very minute holding Callie's strawberry-blond hair back from her furrowed little forehead.

Gregory felt sick. Melissa was no better than Debra. She'd lied to him and used him for her own purposes, with the obvious plan of discarding him once she'd gotten what she wanted. Damn it, he'd *sworn* he would never again let any woman use him. Yet he'd allowed himself to fall for Melissa and she'd hoodwinked him so easily. What a fool he was.

"Please," Callie begged. "We're so worried or my mum never would have sent me to ask."

Gregory stepped out on the veranda. In the corner of the paddock where Ruthie had made her nest he could see a boy holding up a flashlight and a woman kneeling beside the birthing sow. His mind reeled. James's family had been on his property from the beginning. Melissa had known all along.

He set his jaw. "I'll be right out."

MELISSA HEARD CALLIE'S voice and her heart sank. A few more minutes and she would have told Gregory the truth herself. She scrambled to get dressed, hastily pulling on her bra and panties, and cursing Ruthie's bad timing. A few more hours, perhaps, and Constance would have returned. Diane and the kids would have been off the property. Melissa would have been home free.

Gregory appeared in the doorway. One look at his stony face and her heart sank. "I can explain."

"Don't bother, I've figured it out." With jerky movements he flung off his robe and stepped into his jeans, reaching for his T-shirt before he zipped up. "You needed a hiding place for your friend Diane, and my farm was convenient. You used my cottage, my home and my land without my permission, even though you knew James Chalmers was a friend of mine and I'd sworn to do everything I could to help him. You used me—someone who took a chance on you and gave you a job even though you had no qualifications to be a nanny."

Melissa knelt on the floor and groped under the bed for her skirt. "I know it looks bad—"

"Worst of all," he said, his voice tight with anger, "you used my daughter, who loves you and looks up to you. How is Alice Ann going to feel when she finds out you lied to her? Did you even think of that?"

Melissa found her crumpled skirt and stumbled to her feet, holding it in front of her. "I hoped she would never know."

"As you hoped *I* would never know." He yanked his T-shirt over his head, ruffling his dark hair.

"Well, that, too," Melissa admitted.

With a disgusted snort, he turned on his heel.

"Wait just a damn minute!" She lunged after him

and caught him by a belt loop. "Your good mate James was abusing Diane, physically and emotionally." Melissa bunched her fists on her hips. "More recently he hit Callie in the face. I saw the bruises with my own eyes."

"Did you witness him inflict these injuries?" Gregory's voice was as cold as ice.

"No, how could I? But—"

"Then you have no evidence he caused Callie's bruising. Even Diane's alleged injuries are hearsay."

"You're talking like a lawyer!"

"I *am* a lawyer. And one of the first things we learn in law school is that a man is innocent until proven guilty. I've known James Chalmers for fifteen years. There's never been a hint of abuse in his marriage with Diane." Gregory picked Melissa's top off the chair and threw it at her. "I'm going out to see to my sow. You can start packing your bags."

Melissa had never expected to be at the farm long-term, but to be sent packing after a week because she'd tried to help a woman in distress? "Damn right I'm packing. I quit!"

"You can't quit," he barked. "You're fired!"

Melissa started to snap back, but Gregory was already striding down the hall. A second later she heard the screen door slam, followed by his heavy footsteps crossing the veranda. She pulled on her blouse and angrily wiped away a tear. Then she kicked the rumpled bed where they'd made the most incredible love of her entire life. Damn.

Alice Ann appeared in the hall in her Winnie the Pooh nightgown, rubbing her eyes with both fists. "What's that noise outside?"

Melissa came out of Gregory's bedroom and shut the door behind her. She took a deep breath and tried to sound normal. "Ruthie's having her babies."

"Piglets! Let's go see!" Suddenly wide-awake, Alice Ann was all ready to run outside in her nightie and bare feet.

"Whoa!" Melissa said, catching hold of the back of her nightgown. "Put on a jacket and boots. It's cold out there."

"I can't wait to see Ruthie's piglets." Alice Ann wriggled with excitement as Melissa helped her put on a pair of corduroy pants underneath her nightgown. "I wonder how many she'll have."

"Your dad said there's usually at least eight, often ten."

"There were eleven when Benny was born," Alice Ann told her. "That's why he was so small."

"Imagine having ten brothers and sisters," Melissa said, zipping up the child's pink fleece jacket. "You'd never get to watch what you wanted on TV."

"And you'd have to share your toys!" Alice Ann said, wide-eyed. "If your daddy brought you lollies you'd only get one. Or maybe a half."

"Terrible." Melissa smoothed the girl's hair back and impulsively drew her into a hug. Blinking hard, she got to her feet and forced a cheery note into her voice. "Let's go."

The moon had set in the western sky. Dawn was still an hour away and the paddocks were deep in darkness. Alice Ann clung to Melissa's hand as they crunched across the gravel, their breath rising in clouds of steam.

As her eyes adjusted, Melissa could make out Gregory's tall figure standing in the paddock corner where Ruthie had her nest. Flashlight beams bobbed, illuminating small circles of the sow's broad back. When Melissa and Alice Ann got closer, they could see Diane, Josh and Callie hanging over the fence.

Alice Ann stopped short. "They're supposed to be a secret," she whispered.

"They thought Ruthie was in trouble, so Callie came and got your father," Melissa explained, holding tightly to her hand. Would Gregory appreciate the sacrifice Diane had made?

Melissa went to the woman and wordlessly hugged her. Diane clung to her, and when she finally broke free there were tears in her eyes.

"You shouldn't have revealed yourselves," Melissa said in a low voice. "Gregory's really angry. At me, mainly, but it doesn't bode well for you, either."

Her friend's shoulders lifted in a helpless gesture. "I can't hear a creature in pain and not try to do something."

Melissa knew she would have felt the same even though she wasn't a nurse. "What's happening?"

"The sow's very agitated. She keeps getting up and down. One of the piglets was crushed."

Ruthie was swaying on her feet, grunting and panting. Three newborn piglets stumbled around the nest, blindly rooting through the loose grass, searching for their mother's teats. Standing back a ways, Gregory cradled a fourth piglet in his hands. Soft squeaks of pain were the only indication it was still alive.

Alice Ann had joined Callie and Josh. The three children crouched outside the fence and peered through the mesh at the baby pigs.

"Is it badly injured?" Melissa asked quietly.

Gregory moved closer to the fence. His mouth was drawn down in grim lines. "He won't live."

"Oh, no," Melissa groaned. She met Gregory's gaze and for a moment everything else was forgotten. "Is he suffering?"

Gregory gave a curt nod, then moved toward the gate. "I'll take care of it."

"No, Daddy, I'll take care of it." Alice Ann jumped up excitedly. "Remember how I nursed Benny? I'll do the same for this little piggy."

Gregory's face contorted. "It's not the same, sweetheart. This pig is badly injured."

"I can help him." The girl reached out her small arms. "Please, Daddy."

"No," he said harshly, and strode off toward the barn.

"Daddy!" Alice Ann started to run after him.

"Look, Alice Ann!" Melissa caught her girl and turned her back toward Ruthie. "Another baby is coming out. I can see its snout and the tips of the hooves."

Ruthie blundered about her nest, grunting and panting. Her jaw had slackened and a glob of saliva dripped from one yellow tusk.

"Why does she keep moving around?" Diane asked. "She was lying down when she delivered the others."

"She's a first-time mother," Melissa said. "Gregory said sometimes they get nervous."

"Scratch her tummy," Alice Ann suggested. "She always lies down if you scratch her. I'll show you."

"You stay here," Melissa told the girl. "I'll go."

She squeezed through the gate and picked her way to Ruthie, careful not to step on any of the newborn piglets staggering around on wobbly legs. Ruthie's belly was hardened with a contraction, the tough hide covered in coarse black bristles. As Melissa scratched, the pig slowed her restless pacing and finally stopped, but she wouldn't lie down. Melissa kept on scratching. "Lie down, Ruthie," she crooned. "That's a girl."

The sow's front legs started to crumple. She lowered herself to her knees, her hind end a few inches off the ground. There she hovered.

"What's she doing?" Josh wondered.

"Probably making sure there aren't any piglets underneath her," Melissa speculated. She kept scratching. Finally, with a gusty grunt, Ruthie collapsed on her side in her bed of grass, panting.

Melissa held her breath as they waited and watched the baby pig being born. Another contraction from Ruthie pushed the piglet out and onto the grass. Shreds of a thin membrane clung to its glistening body. It lay there a moment, curled in on itself. Then with a jerk, it squirmed and staggered to its feet, only to immediately bump into its mother's haunch and fall over. With a tiny squeal, the newborn got up again and began its search for a teat.

The other three piglets had sniffed out the source of milk and attached themselves to their mother. Ruthie seemed more relaxed now, and in quick succession, five more piglets were born. One by one they completed a circuit or two of their mother before finding their way to a teat. Stacked two high, the rows of piglets nursed in a squirming mass of black-and-white, their tiny tails corkscrewing contentedly.

The eastern sky had lightened to a translucent pearl when they heard Gregory's footsteps behind them. "How's Ruthie?"

Melissa heard the strain in his voice and thought he looked wearier than she'd ever seen him. Despite everything he said about the facts of life on a farm, putting the crushed piglet out of its pain had cost him. She wished she could comfort him, but his expression was too forbidding. Instead, she simply said, "Ruthie has everything under control. She's the proud mother of nine."

Under other circumstances the birth would have brought them together. Now he nodded without so much as a smile. Melissa felt her blood chill with foreboding.

Gregory turned to Diane. "You and your children better come up to the house. I've called James. He's on his way."

CHAPTER FOURTEEN

"OH, NO!" Diane's face turned ashen. "I was afraid something like this would happen." Ignoring Gregory's directive, she put her arms around Josh's and Callie's shoulders and hurried them back to the cottage.

"How could you do that?" Melissa demanded, clenching her fists to stop herself from pummeling him. "You haven't even heard Diane's side of the story."

"I've known James for years. You've known Diane for a week," Gregory said coldly. A muscle jumped in his jaw. "Isn't it just possible that I have more facts than you?"

"You insufferable pig!" Realizing what she'd said, Melissa threw up her hands. "Apologies to Ruthie and the rest."

Gregory started to walk away. "Come, Alice Ann."

"Daddy." Alice Ann tugged at his hand. "Where's the baby pig? Can I see him?"

Gregory's eyes shut briefly. He put a palm on his

daughter's head and in a softer voice said, "I'm sorry, sweetheart. He's dead."

Alice Ann's eyes welled as she soundlessly repeated the dreadful word. She turned to Melissa, who scooped her into her arms. Alice Ann's body shook with sobs. Hot tears filtered through Melissa's hair and slid beneath her collar. Over the little girl's shoulder she threw one last glare at Gregory, who stalked off, whistling for Maxie.

Morning had broken, streaking the sky with pink and blue, but Melissa tucked Alice Ann back into bed. The girl was overwrought with excitement, fatigue and grief, and needed more sleep. She clung to Melissa's hand, not wanting to let go.

"I'll be here when you wake up," Melissa whispered.

"Promise?"

"Cross my heart." She kissed Alice Ann on the forehead, then gently released her grip and pulled up the covers. Then she went back out to the kitchen, where Gregory was putting on the kettle.

"Diane risked her freedom to save your pig, and you sold her out."

"If she's being abused, why doesn't she simply divorce James?" Gregory said.

"You should know it's not always that easy for women," Melissa countered. "She believes James can and will take her children away from her."

"If she really isn't emotionally stable, maybe she shouldn't have custody," Gregory stated. "Remember, she was treated for depression a couple of years ago."

"That was postnatal depression. He threatened to take Josh and Callie away from her, and her parents wouldn't even back her up!" Melissa cried. "She said he would con everyone into believing him, not her. She was right. He's got you fooled into thinking she's unfit to look after her children."

"Why would he do that?"

"Power. He wants to control her."

Gregory shook his head. "Diane's played with your emotions. She's taken advantage of your compassion to gain sympathy for her cause."

"Her *cause* is safety for herself and her children. I don't blame you for being angry at me for lying to you. But don't take it out on her."

He paused, considering. Then he shook his head. "James is my friend. I have to look after his interests."

"Would he still be your friend if he'd abused Diane and Callie?" Melissa demanded.

"I couldn't respect or like a man who did that," Gregory conceded. "But I have to give him the benefit of the doubt."

"Oh, I know where you're coming from," Melissa said, shaking a finger at him. "You don't like that she's taking the children away from James."

"That's right, I don't." Gregory rounded on her, eyes blazing. "No one is allowed to take the law into their own hands."

"Taking control of your life isn't against the law."

"Refusing access to a father is."

"Diane is not Debra and James is not you."

"James cares about those kids."

"James cares about himself. If he's so loving why does he persecute Diane?" Melissa fumed. "Why did he hit Callie?"

For the first time Gregory wavered. "Are you sure about this?"

"Yes!"

He rubbed a hand over his face. "It's too late. James is on his way. He deserves to be heard."

Melissa's shoulders sagged. Bone-weary, she touched her forehead with the heel of her hand. "I told Alice Ann I'd be here when she woke up. I'll leave as soon as I've said goodbye."

She dragged out her suitcases and began to empty the closet, tumbling clothes into the bags at random, a jumble of silky satins and laces mixed in with her jeans and cotton T-shirts. She was furious with Gregory and despairing of herself. She'd tried to do one small thing to help someone, and look how it had backfired! Imagine if she ever tried to do Something Big.

Catching sight of herself in the mirror, she was filled with loathing. There must be *something* more she could do. Her gaze dropped to the dresser—

Of course! What hadn't she thought of that right away?

Melissa grabbed her car keys and ran quickly

down the hall. Gregory wasn't in the kitchen. She slipped out through the screen door, closing it carefully so it didn't bang, and sprinted across the yard to the cottage. She didn't knock, just turned the handle. It was locked. "Diane? It's me."

Diane opened the door a crack, just enough for Melissa to enter. Her eyes were dry and there was a determined jut to her chin. "James is not going to collect me like some parcel at the post office. I'll barricade the door. I'll wait him out until Constance gets back."

"That won't work. Gregory's bound to have a key." Melissa pressed her car keys into Diane's hand. "Take my car. About five kilometers down Balderdash Road, take a left onto the side road. My parents' house is called Heronwood." It didn't matter what Cheryl and Tony thought or did now; Diane's options had run out. "You'll be safe there."

Diane hesitated, anxiously jiggling the keys. "I haven't driven a stick shift in years. I'm better here, where it's safe."

"You're not thinking clearly. You have to get away. I'd go with you, but I promised Alice Ann I'd be here when she woke up." Melissa pushed her toward the door. "Josh, Callie," she called over her shoulder. "You're leaving now."

"What if I meet James on the road?"

"You drive straight to the police station," Melissa told her. "When you get there, call me on my mobile phone."

Diane shut her eyes. When she opened them, she nodded grimly. "You're right. We have to go. Come on, kids."

Warily, Josh peeked around the corner. "Is *he* here?"

"Not yet," Diane said. "Melissa's lending us her car and we're going to her parents' house."

"It's okay," Josh called to his sister. "Come on."

The two children came out, holding hands and wearing their backpacks. Melissa's heart ached for them, for their loss of innocence and for their bravery. "Run and get in the car," she urged them. "Everything's going to be fine."

"Thank you," Diane said, hugging her. "Aren't you coming, too?"

"I want to see Alice Ann once more."

"But how will you get home without your car?"

"I'll call my sister for a lift. I'll see you very soon," Melissa promised, waving them off. "Don't let Tony sell you anything."

Diane and the kids ran across the barnyard to where the Volkswagen was parked at the side of the house. They scrambled inside. A moment later the engine roared to life.

The front door of the house opened and Gregory stepped onto the veranda.

"Take the lane!" Melissa called to Diane as an afterthought. James would likely arrive soon and would undoubtedly come up the drive. But the Volkswagen's windows were up and Diane couldn't hear. With a spurt of gravel, she shot off down the driveway. Melissa bounced on her toes, hugging herself with the tension. They were getting away—

And then over the rise in the driveway came a late-model, black Mercedes-Benz. Melissa uttered a strangled cry and clutched her head. The Volkswagen slowed as the two cars approached each other head-on. With a fence on one side and the pine trees on the other, there was no room to pass. The vehicles stopped, facing each other.

"I can't believe this," Melissa muttered. "Back up!" She waved her arms and jumped up and down, trying to attract Diane's attention. "Go around by the lane."

After an agonizing moment of inaction, that's exactly what Diane started to do. The Volkswagen jerked backward a couple of yards, stuttered…and died.

Melissa groaned. Diane had taken her foot off the clutch too soon! The engine cranked over again. But now the door of the Mercedes was opening. James got out, shouting and cursing at his wife. Suddenly Melissa was terrified for her friend. It was one thing to know in the abstract that Diane's husband had abused her; it was quite another to see a powerfully built man with a history of violence charging at a defenseless woman.

Melissa ran toward the cars, screaming at Gregory to stop James. Gregory walked slowly down the steps, as if he couldn't quite believe the evidence of his own eyes.

The Volkswagen's engine cranked repeatedly, but didn't catch. James grabbed the handle of the driver-side door and tried to wrench it open. When he found it was locked, he banged his fist on the roof, denting the metal.

Melissa caught a glimpse of Callie's terrified face through a back window before the girl dived for the floor. James's other fist connected with Diane's window and cracked it.

Gregory's mouth dropped open. Then he ran toward the Volkswagen.

The engine finally turned over. Diane started to reverse jerkily, swerving wildly. James ran after her, cursing and shouting, battering the hood of the vehicle whenever he was close enough. She got the car under control and increased her speed. Melissa dodged to avoid being run over as the Beetle came to a skidding stop, then spun toward the lane. James could have run back to his car and overtaken his wife in minutes, but he seemed crazed. He lunged after her on foot, yelling curses that made Melissa want to cover her ears.

Suddenly he stopped. At first she thought he'd given up because Diane was pulling away. Then Melissa realized something was dreadfully wrong. His face had turned an alarming shade of purple and had swollen, as if engorged with rage. The next few seconds seemed to happen in slow motion. His eyes wide and bulging, James clutched his chest, pulling at his shirt. He staggered a few steps, fell heavily to his knees, then collapsed facedown on the gravel.

Gregory was at James's side before Melissa. He turned the man over onto his back, putting an ear to his heart, fingertips to his carotid artery. Gregory glanced up at Melissa. "His heart has stopped. Call emergency."

She whipped her mobile phone out of her pocket and, with trembling fingers, punched in the numbers.

Diane scrambled out of the car, her face white. "Is he dead?"

"He had a heart attack," Gregory told her.

James lay inert, arms outstretched, face gray, his pale eyes staring up at the sky, unseeingly.

Melissa felt like throwing up. She put an arm around Diane and tried to lead her away. Gregory loosened James's tie and started giving him mouth-to-mouth resuscitation.

Diane broke away from Melissa and dropped to her knees beside her husband, pushing Gregory out of the way. Raising her clasped hands above her head, she brought them down with a resounding thump on James's chest. His legs bounced off the ground.

"Bastard! I wish you were dead!" she screamed, and hit him again. Melissa heard James's sternum crack, and flinched. She'd read that that could happen, that too often people didn't press hard enough, but the sound was shocking.

"Stop it. You're killing him!" Gregory said, alarmed. "You don't want to go to jail over the man."

"She's giving him CPR." Melissa took off her cardigan to fold under James's head as a make-shift pillow.

"Thank goodness. I'll get a blanket from the house." Gregory ran off.

Diane compressed James's chest a few more times, then felt for his carotid artery. "I've got a pulse." She plugged his nose and blew into his mouth. After a few breaths, she put her cheek to his nostrils. "He's still not breathing."

She took another breath and bent to recommence mouth-to-mouth. Suddenly her face turned a sickly green. "I'm going to throw up," she announced matter-of-factly. "You have to take over."

"Me? No way!" Melissa held up her hands and backed away. "I'm no good at sickness and injury. No good at all."

"You know how. Just do it." Diane staggered to her feet and lurched to the fence, where she began to retch.

Just do it. Melissa glanced toward the house. Gregory was nowhere in sight. Diane was throwing up. James was not breathing. Fear was making Melissa's own heart jump around like a caged animal, and sweat had popped out along her hairline. But she had no choice.

Kneeling beside James, she pinched his nostrils shut and placed her mouth over his to form an airtight seal. Her obsessive reading of first-aid books came back to her. She refused to dwell on who he was and what he'd done to Diane. He was a human being and it was up to *her* to save him. No, she couldn't think about *that* or she'd start freaking out again. *Blow, check for rising chest. Blow, check for breathing.* She fell into a rhythm. Blow and check. Blow and check.

She didn't know how long she gave James mouth-to-mouth resuscitation. Gregory came and laid a blanket over him, then brought Diane a bottle of water and led her away to sit inside the Volkswagen with Callie and Josh. Melissa was so intent on what she was doing she didn't hear the sirens until they were turning into the driveway. Still, she didn't quit. Blow and check. Blow and check. Blow—

Gregory gripped her shoulder and gently pulled her away. Paramedics in dark blue shirts and black slacks took her place. A plump blond woman put an oxygen mask over James's face while a balding man swiftly checked his vital signs. They transferred him to a stretcher and carried him into the ambulance, where he was put on a drip.

Diane told the blond woman she was a nurse and briefly gave them the facts of James's collapse, avoiding mention of the circumstances surrounding the incident. After making notes, the paramedic glanced from Melissa to Diane. "Are either of you his next of kin?"

Diane turned even paler than she already was. "I'm his wife."

"He's going to be all right, ma'am," the blonde assured her. "Would you like to ride in the ambulance?"

Diane hesitated, glancing toward the Volkswagen. "My children…"

Melissa could feel Diane's revulsion at the thought of being trapped in there with James, even if he was unconscious. "It'll be all right. I'll take Josh and Callie and follow you to the hospital."

Diane nodded, resigned. "I'll see you there."

The paramedic seemed to think Diane needed additional reassurance. "He's very lucky you're a trained nurse and that you were on the spot. He might not have survived, otherwise."

Diane looked at Melissa. No words were necessary. Melissa didn't know whether to laugh or to cry. She pulled her friend into a hug and held her, patting her as if she were a child. "You did the right thing. You are truly amazing."

Diane eased away, wiping at her eyes. "I'm not crazy."

"I know you're not." Melissa suddenly had a feeling Diane was going to be just fine. James, she wasn't so sure about.

As for Melissa, as the ambulance pulled away, pieces clicked into place in her brain, and suddenly she could see her future with startling clarity.

CHAPTER FIFTEEN

YOU NEVER REALLY KNEW a man until you'd seen him attack a Volkswagen Beetle. Gregory stared after the ambulance carrying his former friend, Judge James Chalmers, then turned to Melissa. Somehow he didn't feel quite the same level of righteous anger toward her as he had half an hour ago. "Are you okay?"

"I'm fine." She was even-tempered but brisk. "I'll take Josh and Callie to the hospital."

Something was different about her, but Gregory couldn't put his finger on what. She was shell-shocked, he presumed. Even though there'd been no blood, witnessing James having a heart attack had to be traumatic for her. "You shouldn't drive. Come with me and Alice Ann in my car."

"No," Melissa said slowly, "I'll go on my own."

"I'll see you there." He turned to go back to the house, and almost tripped over Alice Ann in her nightgown and blue gum boots.

"Who was that man lying on the ground?" she asked.

"James Chalmers, Callie and Josh's father. He

had a heart attack, but he's alive and the doctors and nurses will take good care of him." Gregory took her hand. "Let's get you dressed. We'll go see him in the hospital."

Melissa had left by the time Gregory and Alice Ann started out. They were halfway to Ballarat when Alice Ann said, "He hit Melissa's car."

"He was angry," Gregory said, realizing she must have seen everything.

"That's no excuse to hurt something."

Gregory winced, recognizing his own words. "No, it's not."

He was still having trouble reconciling the respected Judge Chalmers with the lunatic who'd gone after Melissa's car. Not Melissa's car—*Diane*. Gregory shifted uncomfortably.

"He hurt Callie," Alice Ann told him. "He squeezed her arm really hard and then he hit her on the forehead."

Gregory frowned into the rearview mirror. Harsh life lessons were being thrown at his daughter from all directions and he couldn't protect her from any of them. "Who told you that?"

"Callie. When you were talking to the ambulance man." Alice Ann was quiet a moment, then said, "Her daddy's a bad man, isn't he?"

"If what Callie says is true, then, yes, he's a bad man. But everyone's innocent until proven guilty." Although Gregory had to admit the evidence against James was damning.

A half hour later he was standing at his bedside in intensive care. James was groggy, slipping in and out of consciousness. His skin was ashen, his face still swollen. Tubes ran out of him to drips and collecting bags. Wires hooked him up to machines that flashed digital readouts of blood pressure and oxygen-saturation levels. A jagged red line across a monitor screen registered his erratic heartbeat.

"How long will it take him to recover?" Gregory asked the ICU nurse, a woman in her forties with short brown hair. He'd already learned that Diane, her kids and Melissa had come in, seen James briefly, then left for the hospital's coffee shop.

"It's hard to say," the nurse replied. "Once he's stabilized he'll have tests to see how much trauma was done to his heart and whether he sustained brain damage."

"Brain damage!"

"Due to oxygen deprivation while his heart wasn't beating," she said dispassionately. "I wouldn't worry yet. I understand he was resuscitated quickly."

"Daddy?" Alice Ann tugged on his hand. "Can we go? I want to see Melissa."

Gregory rubbed the back of his neck. Melissa. Now he was going to pay for being an idiot and not listening to her about Diane's safety. Telling Alice Ann about the abattoir suddenly seemed a small thing compared with admitting he'd fired her favorite nanny.

Gregory touched his friend on the shoulder. "I'll be back."

The judge grunted and tried to lift his head.

"Did you say something?"

"Nee'…you…help." James labored to make himself understood.

"Do you want me to get Diane and the kids?"

He ponderously moved his head sideways. *No.* "She…can't…leave…me." He shut his eyes in exhaustion. After a moment he opened them again and Gregory saw in them a brief flash of the piercing focus he had once so admired. "Tell…her… lose…Josh, Callie."

"I can't say that. I won't." Gregory felt sickened by what he was hearing. "You're not yourself. You should rest."

"S'preme…Cour'…seat…ridin'…this," James persisted. "Do…whatever. Threaten…doctor… her…unfit." James squeezed his hand. "*You* do… for…me."

Appalled, Gregory withdrew it. "James, I have to go. We'll talk when you're feeling better. The best advice I can give you, as a friend and as a lawyer, is once you've recovered to get counseling for your anger-management problem."

Melissa was sitting with Diane and her children in a sunny corner of the coffee shop. While Gregory waited at the cashier to pay for Alice Ann's toast and milk, he studied Melissa across the room. She looked calm, and *different* in some indefinable way.

More sure of herself? She rarely looked away from Diane, and then only to speak to Josh or Callie, squeezing a hand here, smoothing a lock of hair there.

Gregory carried his tray over to their table. All four were wary. "May Alice Ann sit with you?" he asked Diane.

"Of course." She made room to pull up another chair.

"I'd like to talk to you, Melissa," Gregory said. "Privately."

She exchanged a glance with Diane, then got up and followed him to another table a few yards away.

"You were right. I was wrong," Gregory said. Eating humble pie wasn't so much painful as embarrassing. He had to apologize and do it quickly, before he lost her. "I don't know how I could have been so mistaken about someone I've known for years, someone I respected and admired, but I was. I'm sorry I didn't listen to you."

Melissa stared at him, unblinking, perfectly composed. "Is that all?"

"No, there's more." Gregory paused, afraid of what she might say when he asked her to stay. "You're not fired. I want you to come back to work."

"Oh, I fully intend to," Melissa said with a brittle smile he didn't recognize.

"I beg your pardon?" He half expected to have to convince her.

"I promised you I'd commit to being Alice Ann's nanny for at least three months, and I don't go back on my word."

"Oh. Good." He didn't know quite what to say.

"I apologize for lying to you," she continued. "However, I want you to know I never lied to Alice Ann. And I didn't steal from you. Every morsel of food Diane and her kids ate was paid for out of my pocket, not yours."

"That's not important," he said uncomfortably.

"James froze their bank account and canceled her credit card," Melissa explained. "She didn't have a cent to her name."

Gregory massaged his temples. His head was beginning to throb from the effort of continually adjusting his outdated image of his friend. Best to move on for now. "About our arrangements—"

"I'll move into the cottage as soon as it's cleared out and ready. Until then I'll sleep at my parents," Melissa informed him. "Once I'm at the farm I'll stay out of your way and you'll stay out of mine. It's Alice Ann's welfare we ought to be concerned about, not our feelings."

She might have taken the words right out of his mouth. He felt a small surge of relief. She wasn't leaving them completely. "It'll be awkward."

"You'll hardly ever see me," she said. "We can communicate by e-mail once I bring my computer over."

Disappointment came hard on the heels of his relief. "Do we need to go to those lengths?"

"On weekends I'll go to my parents' house," Melissa continued, as if he hadn't spoken. "In a week you'll forget I exist except as the nanny and housekeeper."

She was proposing a businesslike association firmly focused on his daughter's welfare. Exactly what he'd had in mind when he'd hired a nanny. He should be glad. "Anything else?"

"I'll need time off to attend classes," she said. "I don't know how much yet, or at what times."

"What are you going to study?"

Melissa's sudden smile caught him by surprise. "I'm going to be a nurse."

"A *nurse?*" He laughed, certain he hadn't heard her right. "You can't stand the sight of blood."

"That's a drawback," she conceded, "but I'll just have to get over it."

"When did you decide this?"

"As James was being taken away in the ambulance. I should have figured it out long ago, but my squeamishness threw me." Melissa leaned forward. "I know a lot about injury and illness. My family thinks it's because I'm a hypochondriac. The truth is, I find medicine interesting. Plus, I enjoy taking care of people. Even James. I can't quite describe the feeling of knowing I helped save a man's life." She squared her shoulders and spread her hands wide. "I wanted to do Something

Big. What could be bigger than helping sick people get well again?"

"Why not be a doctor?"

Melissa shook her head. "Nurses have the nurturing relationship with the patients. That appeals to me."

Gregory sat back and gazed across the table at her. "So that's what's different. You finally know what you want."

"Isn't it wonderful?"

"Just do yourself one favor."

"What's that?" she asked warily.

"See a doctor about your thumb."

The latest Band-Aid had come off, exposing her red and swollen digit. "*Yes*. I knew it was bad. No one else thought so."

Gregory chuckled. He was going to miss the laughter and the easy conversation with her, the moments of pure silliness. This past week had been so full of promise he'd started thinking beyond the immediate present, to the future. Hopefully, she simply needed space and time to realize he wasn't such a bad guy, after all.

"About last night…" he began, frowning as he tried to figure out how best to word this. He wanted to keep their options open, while not pressuring her to commit to him until she was ready.

Melissa's smile faded as he continued to hesitate. "That was a mistake," she finally said. "*I* was on the rebound. *You've* been too long out of circulation.

We had a physical attraction, that's all. In every way, we're too different. Everything happened so fast we didn't have time to figure that out." She was coming up with so many empty reasons, her voice had become strained. As if she realized that, she pushed herself out of her chair. "Let's call it quits while we're ahead."

Gregory was stunned at how swiftly and ruthlessly she'd disposed of them. Everything she'd said was true, except that there *was* more to their relationship than mere physical attraction. Much more.

Dazed, he nodded, aware of a heavy, dull feeling in his chest. When she became a nurse, would she be able to fix a broken heart?

As MELISSA, DIANE AND THE kids passed Constance's house on the way home from the hospital, Diane glanced at her friend's empty driveway, then sat back, disappointed but resigned. "She's not home yet."

"She might not get back until late. Tonight my parents will put you up," Melissa said. "You guys can use Ally's old room."

"Are you sure they won't mind?"

"Not a bit," Melissa said. "But we'd better swing by the cottage to pick up the blankets."

She pulled up in front, relieved to see that Gregory wasn't back yet. She'd had enough drama for one day. Diane ran in for the blankets, leaving Melissa to wait with the car running.

She glanced in the rearview mirror, saw that Josh and Callie were both asleep, and fell to brooding about her immediate future. Was she insane to think she could live at the farm after everything that had happened between her and Gregory? But she simply couldn't abandon Alice Ann so abruptly, especially not when Benny was still on the chopping block, so to speak.

Diane came out with the folded blankets and got back in the car. Within five minutes Melissa turned off onto the side road that led to Heronwood, a two-story Victorian set on a couple of acres. Cheryl met them at the door and instantly began clucking over Josh and Callie as if she were a rather elegant mother hen and they were a pair of stray chicks.

"Come in, darlings," she said, opening the door wider. "There's milk and cake for you in the kitchen. Straight ahead down the hall. Off you go." She turned and extended an arm to Diane. "You poor thing. I couldn't believe it when Melissa told me what you've been through, sleeping in that dank old cottage with no heat or electricity."

"Thank you for lending us the blankets," Diane said, holding the bundle to her chest. "I appreciate it."

"I wish Melissa had told me what they were really for." Cheryl cast a reproachful look at her daughter. "I would have sent along sheets, as well."

Diane sighed. "I dream of sheets."

"Tonight you shall sleep on Egyptian cotton,

four hundred and fifty thread count." Cheryl beckoned her down the hall. "I'll show you to your room."

Melissa left her mother to make Diane at home, and went through to the kitchen, where she found her sister giving Josh and Callie a piece of chocolate cake and a glass of milk each.

"I heard about what happened from Mother, and came over to see if there was anything I could do," Ally said. "Want a slice?" she added, cutting another one.

"Thanks." About to reach for her cake, Melissa paused to say hello to Tony, who'd just come in from the backyard. "I've come home for a few days and brought some houseguests."

"So I heard," he replied, deftly scooping up Melissa's serving of cake, oblivious to her aggrieved expression. "So how's that farmer of yours? When are you going to marry him?"

Cheryl walked into the room. Hearing this last remark, she shot her husband a warning glance. "Darling!"

"When pigs fly," Melissa replied to Tony. Her dad obviously hadn't heard the whole story, which she had briefly related to her mother over the phone. Feeling desperate for some chocolate, Melissa nodded at Ally to cut her another piece of cake.

Her sister pushed the knife through the rich fudge icing and moist layers. She'd just placed the piece on a plate and was handing it to Melissa when

Diane came into the room. "Want some?" she asked, offering it to her instead.

"Thank you," Diane said. "This looks beautiful."

Melissa groaned softly as her sister cut another slice and gave it to Cheryl. Then Ally cut the remaining wedge in two and plunked the pieces on Josh's and Callie's plates. "There you go."

"Hey!" Melissa squawked. She pinched a few crumbs from the empty plate.

Callie glanced at her with big blue eyes and pushed her plate over. "I've already had some."

"Are you sure?" Melissa said.

Callie nodded solemnly. "You're my hero."

Melissa blinked. A week ago she would have been scared silly if anyone had burdened her with such a label. Now…well, she hardly considered herself a hero, but neither was she afraid of other people's expectations. "Thanks, Callie. You're a great kid."

"I understand your husband is Judge Chalmers," Tony was saying to Diane. "Melissa told us of your troubles. His name rang a bell that day we saw him on the news and now I've remembered why. He fined me five thousand dollars a few years back for nothing."

Cheryl rolled her eyes. "You were selling furniture from Thailand without an import license."

"A simple misunderstanding over the complex rules of international trade, my dear," Tony said, brushing her comment aside. "A judge has the discretion to dismiss trivial matters, but Chalmers took an unreasonable dislike to me." He smiled cheerily. "Can't imagine why."

"All that's in the past, thank goodness," Ally said, and turned to Diane. "The question is, what are you going to do now?"

"I'm not going back to Ballarat," she replied firmly. "I'd like to stay in Tipperary Springs."

Ally went to the sideboard and got a notepad out of her purse. "We might as well start making a list of things you'll need to get sorted out—school, doctor, place to live…."

"Melissa has plans, too," Diane said.

Everyone turned to her expectantly.

Melissa finished the last bite of her cake and sat up. Her family was supportive, but they weren't going to believe she could do this. "I'm going to be a nurse."

Sure enough, Cheryl, Tony and Ally exchanged glances.

"*You, a nurse?*" Ally said politely.

"That's right." Melissa lifted her chin. "Don't anyone try to talk me out of it. Or say I can't do it. I'm going to be the best bloody nurse you've ever seen."

"Speaking of which, what *about* the blood?" Ally asked.

"You hate the stuff," Cheryl reminded her.

Even Tony grimaced. "Could be a stumbling block."

"Will everyone quit carrying on about the

blood?" Melissa demanded. "If I can give a heart-attack victim artificial resuscitation, I can cope with a little bleeding."

There was an astonished silence while everyone took this in. Finally Ally said, "You revived a heart-attack victim?"

"Not all by myself," Melissa admitted.

"She was amazing," Diane said. "He wouldn't have survived if not for her."

Ally was the first to understand Melissa was serious. "I always knew that when you figured out what you wanted to do with your life you'd tackle it head-on."

Cheryl put her arm around Melissa's shoulders. "It makes perfect sense when I think of how you used to continually bandage poor Winston's paw even when it wasn't sore." To Diane she explained, "Winston was our late bulldog, rest his soul."

"This calls for champagne." Tony got up to bring a bottle from the fridge.

They toasted to the future and new lives. Tony had cracked a second bottle, a chardonnay, when Ben and Danny arrived. Ally had called Ben, and he'd brought roasted pumpkin soup and sourdough bread from Mangos. Cheryl made a salad and they all sat down to an impromptu feast.

By eight o'clock, the fatigue and stress was starting to show on the runaways. Josh and Callie were practically asleep in their soup bowls and Diane was repeatedly stifling yawns.

"Get some rest," Melissa advised. "First thing to-morrow, we'll find you a good lawyer."

"I forgot to tell you," Diane said. "Gregory gave me his card as we were leaving the hospital. He offered to represent me free of charge."

"Are you going to let him?" Melissa asked, surprised and pleased that Gregory was trying to make practical amends to Diane.

Diane lifted her shoulders. "I have no money of my own, and until I do, I'd be a fool not to accept his generous offer. Of course, I'll pay back every cent as soon as I can." Then she grinned crookedly. "James always said Gregory Finch was the best custody lawyer in the state."

Melissa smiled at the irony, but her heart was sore. Even though she and Gregory were now on the same side of that dispute, as far as their relationship went they were further apart than ever. In the hospital cafeteria she'd waited for him to contradict her, hoping he would tell her he loved her and wanted her back, not just as a nanny but as his lover and his friend. He hadn't. She could only conclude that he hadn't forgiven her for deceiving him, even though it was for a good cause. He'd made it very clear that as far as he was concerned, they didn't have a future.

GREGORY DROVE HOME from the hospital, his thoughts circling around Melissa. She might have been justified in hiding Diane, but she'd still lied to him and used him. He could forgive, but it wouldn't be easy to forget. Had she been pretending when she'd made love to him, too?

"Where's the baby pig that died?" Alice Ann asked suddenly, from the backseat.

Gregory started. She'd been so quiet on the way home he'd thought she'd gone to sleep. He had to think a moment about where he'd put the piglet. "In the barn. I'll bury it when we get home."

"We'll have a funeral for him," Alice Ann said. "Melissa will help me pick flowers."

"She'll probably be busy with other things. She's moving into the cottage." As soon as he got home he was going to call up a moving company and get them to come and take the extra furniture away. He should have done that in the first place instead of trying to do everything himself.

"She'll want to be there," Alice Ann said confidently.

Gregory slowed to turn into the driveway. A lifetime seemed to have passed since he'd woken up with Melissa in his bed in the predawn dark. It had only been eight days since he'd first laid eyes on her. Unbelievably, in that short time she'd burrowed deep beneath his skin, into his mind and into his heart. He had to keep reminding himself that whatever madness they'd had was *over.*

He crested the rise in the driveway, his gaze automatically seeking out Melissa's Volkswagen. It wasn't there. She must have taken Diane and her children someplace else.

He parked at the back of the house and sat for a moment, his hands gripping the steering wheel. There was the cottage where she would sleep at night. There was his house, where she would play with his daughter, who would regale him every night with stories of "Melissa did this, Melissa said that."

How the hell was he going to forget the woman if she wouldn't go away?

CHAPTER SIXTEEN

MELISSA'S PERFUME lingered on the air every evening when Gregory came home from work, tantalizing him with traces of her presence. Tonight, the kitchen was also filled with the aroma of chicken and mushrooms from the casserole heating in the oven. The house was tidy, the laundry done and the bathrooms clean. One month after she'd moved into the cottage, his life was orderly and running smoothly. Yet it seemed emptier than it had been even before she'd come to Finch Farm. Her influence was everywhere, but Melissa herself was always just out of reach.

The squirming bundle of soft tawny fur under Gregory's arm wriggled free, and the golden retriever puppy plopped onto the kitchen floor in a sprawling heap. He let out a tiny yip of surprise at finding himself in unfamiliar territory.

"Alice Ann!" Gregory called, knowing she wouldn't be far away.

"Hi, Daddy," she called, running in from the

veranda. "Guess what Benny did—" She stopped when she saw the puppy, her eyes widening.

"Hey, sweetheart," Gregory said. "What do you think of your new pet?"

"Mine?" She crouched and the puppy ambled over to lick her hand. He had soft brown fur and a round belly, and wiggled energetically, wagging his short feathery tail. "What's his name?"

"Whatever you decide," Gregory said.

Alice Ann gathered the puppy into her lap. He stood on his hind legs and planted his paws on her chest to lick her face. She laughed and struggled to hold on to the squirming bundle of soft fur. "I'll call him Wriggles."

"That's a good name." Gregory went back to the car to get the bag of puppy chow he'd bought on the way home. As he shut the car door he caught the swirling wisp of a full skirt disappearing into the cottage.

That's all he saw of Melissa these days— glimpses in the distance as he drove off in the morning or when he tended the pigs in the evening. Their communication had been reduced to notes left on the kitchen counter or e-mails sent from her laptop to his work computer. He never spoke to her or saw her up close. She'd spend the day with Alice Ann, then leave the house as soon as his car turned into the driveway. There was always a meal prepared and left in the oven, timed to be ready fifteen minutes after he arrived home. He suspected Diane, who he knew had moved in with Constance, was still doing the cooking.

"We'll need these two bowls," Gregory instructed Alice Ann, grabbing them from the cupboard. "One for food, the other for water." He filled the water bowl, then showed Alice Ann how much dry food to scoop out for Wriggles.

With the puppy fed, Gregory went to the fridge for a cold beer and saw the note from Melissa. "Sorry, no eggs. Constance wasn't in. I'll get some tomorrow." He ran his fingers over the paper. She never wanted to let him down on anything.

"I'm going next door for eggs," he said to Alice Ann. "You'd better come, too."

"Can I bring Wriggles?" Alice Ann rolled a ball across the kitchen floor for the puppy to run after.

"Attach a lead to his collar," Gregory said. "We don't want to spend all our time chasing him."

Constance returned home late in the evening on the day James had his heart attack. The following afternoon Gregory had been out in the paddock, notching the new piglets' ears, when Melissa's Volkswagen had pulled into Constance's yard, bringing Diane and her children to stay. Melissa had gone inside with them and stayed for several hours. Gregory imagined the three women sitting around Constance's breakfast table, drinking coffee and filling each other in on the drama of their lives.

The journey across the barnyard now was painfully slow, with Wriggles stopping to investigate every dandelion and fence post. Gregory's eyes went continually to the cottage. He could hear the faint sound of a country-music ballad. The Volkswagen parked out front had had the dent in the roof repaired and the broken window replaced. Alice Ann wanted to stop and show Wriggles to Melissa, but Gregory didn't want to disturb her in the evening. Her time was her own, much as he would have liked to see her and talk to her himself.

In Constance's orchard the leaves were turning color and the sweet scent of overripe fruit hung in the cool air. The long autumn was drawing to a close. Laughter came from the leafy branches, and he looked up. Callie and Josh had abandoned the pile of windfalls they were collecting to climb the tree. They waved at Alice Ann and beckoned her over.

"Can I go show them Wriggles, Daddy?"

When he nodded, she ran off with the puppy bounding along behind her, his ears and tail flying.

Constance was in the chicken pen, shooing her flock into their roost for the night. She wore black rubber boots, jeans and a pale purple polo shirt that had faded around the hem. The hens clucked and squawked, beating their russet-brown wings, churning up the dust. Finally they were all inside and she shut the coop door.

"Do you want eggs?" she asked, joining Gregory.

"Yes," he said. "I guess Melissa missed seeing you today."

"I was in and out of the house all day." As his neighbor led the way across the yard, she glanced to the orchard, where Josh and Callie had come down from the tree to pat Wriggles. "Nice looking pup. Alice Ann must be thrilled."

"I got him hoping to distract her from Benny," Gregory confessed. "I've delayed sending the pig to the abattoir as long as possible, but he'll have to go with the next batch of weaners, in a few weeks."

"I know how attached your daughter is to that pig," Constance stated. "A dog was a good idea."

"Even with Wriggles to take her mind off Benny's demise, she's going to be upset," Gregory said. His dread over Alice Ann's impending heartache hadn't diminished with her knowing Benny's fate; if anything, it had intensified.

"Melissa was saying the other day how worried she was about Alice Ann's feelings," Constance told him. "So I've been thinking. If you like, I'll take Benny from you. I enjoy animals and I've got plenty of space. Alice Ann could come over anytime to visit him."

Gregory stopped short, not sure he'd heard correctly. "Do you really mean that?"

"Alice Ann is a sweetheart. And I'm pretty impressed with her father, too." Constance gave him a warm smile. "It's wonderful what you're doing for Diane."

"I'm glad to help," Gregory said. "James's behavior came as a huge shock. I guess you know that Diane filed for divorce."

"And James retaliated by applying for sole custody of Josh and Callie," Constance said, her mouth twisting in a grimace of disgust. "He won't get away with that, will he?"

"Not a chance," Gregory said. "He knows it, too. He's simply harassing her through the courts in an attempt to cause her the maximum distress."

"He's out of the hospital, did you know?" Constance stepped off the gravel onto the short concrete path leading to the back of the house.

"I hadn't heard," Gregory said. "All my communication with James is through his lawyers."

She kicked aside pairs of boots to clear a path to the door. "Melissa told me he goes twice a week for rehab. I gather they've ruled out brain damage, but in my opinion the man's always had a screw loose."

"How *is* Melissa?" Gregory asked casually. "What's she doing?"

"She volunteers through a charity organization to visit patients at the hospital." Constance looked at him, puzzled. "Didn't she mention it?"

"We don't talk much," he admitted. "Ships passing in the night and all that."

"Pity. She's a tonic for anyone. And you seem to be working too much, as usual." Constance turned the door handle. "Wait here. I'll get those eggs."

Hearing Wriggles bark, Gregory glanced to the

orchard to check on Alice Ann. She was helping the other children gather apples. Constance was right, Gregory thought, watching them absently. He *was* working too hard. He used to meet friends in the city for dinner or the theater, or go to his partners' houses in Tipperary Springs for a barbecue on the weekend. Now he stayed at home, played with Alice Ann until she went to bed, then did paperwork until he was too exhausted to think. He was burying his problems in work instead of trying to fix them.

The back door opened again and Constance handed him a carton with a dozen eggs. She waved away the coins he pulled out of his pocket. "You deserve them, working for Diane pro bono."

"Now that she's gone back to nursing, she wants to start paying me." Gregory smiled. "I told her her cooking was payment enough."

Constance laughed heartily. "Melissa said we wouldn't be able to fool you."

Gregory looked away, his smile fading. "She fooled me for a while."

"She talks about you."

"She does?" he tried to glean every nuance of meaning from Constance's face and tone.

Her expression was sympathetic, but her words offered little hope. "She says she can't go back to the way things were."

Gregory tightened his jaw. Would Melissa ever be ready to renew their relationship? Or would she simply move away when her three months were up and her obligation to him and Alice Ann fulfilled?

"I'd better get home," he said. "Thank you for taking Benny. It'll mean the world to Alice Ann. I can't tell you how much I appreciate it."

Impulsively, Constance squeezed his arm. "*Talk* to Melissa. You two will never work anything out by avoiding each other."

"You said she didn't want to go back to the way things were."

"Use your brain," his neighbor said with a smile. "There's more than one way for people to be together."

Thoughtfully, Gregory tucked his egg carton under his arm. "I'll see what I can come up with."

MELISSA SAT at the elderly patient's bedside and held his hand while Diane removed wads of gauze saturated with blood and pus from his backside. Mr. Emerson had been admitted to hospital two days ago, from a nursing home, with deeply infected bedsores.

"Almost done." She smiled reassuringly and hoped she wouldn't faint from the sight and smell. She patted his hand and forced herself to watch. And learn.

She tried whenever she could to be at the hospital when Diane was on duty, because she explained things to Melissa that the other nurses considered volunteers didn't need to know.

"Last one." Diane set the kidney-shaped bowl aside and took ointment and fresh dressings from the trolley. "Have you heard back from the nursing school about your application?"

"Not yet." Melissa stood so she could watch Diane flush the wound with sterile saline solution. "It's been two months since I applied, and I've been on tenterhooks ever since. The letter's got to come soon if I'm going to start with the midyear intake of students."

"It'll come," Diane assured her. "You're going to make a great nurse, I can tell already."

Melissa swelled with pride. Diane's praise meant a lot to her, even though so far it was only based on her rapport with the patients. She admired Diane's quiet confidence as she went about her job, and hoped that someday she could do as well. "What's the latest with James?"

"He's still saying he wants me to come home," Diane told her. "He begs and pleads and promises never to hurt me or the kids again."

"Oh, Diane," she said, dismayed. "You're not going, are you?"

"Never," her friend replied, her mouth set in a firm line. "I've heard it all before. He's refused counseling and anger-management classes. Why should I believe he'll ever change?" She looked up, her eyes dry but her expression sorrowful. "I lost whatever love I had for him long ago."

"Time away helps you see more clearly," Melissa

sympathized. Just as time away from Gregory had helped her see just how much she loved him. *Too late.* Every day got a little lonelier. He didn't telephone, never tried to see her. He was content with e-mails and scribbled notes.

Diane taped the dressing in place and pulled down Mr. Emerson's hospital gown. Then she adjusted his pillows and said loudly, "All done for now, Mr. Emerson. I'll be back in an hour to turn you."

Melissa put his glass of water within reach. "I'll come and read to you later."

Mr. Emerson's seamed face creased in a weak smile as he quavered, "Thank you."

Melissa and Diane left the ward and walked down the hall toward the nurses' station. Melissa was eager for news about Gregory, but didn't want to appear too anxious. "Has Gregory been able to stop James from harassing you?"

"He's written to the state judicial council recommending that James be taken off the short list for the Supreme Court," Diane said. "If James knows he has no chance of being appointed, then he's got no motive to gain custody of the kids. I know he loves them—in spite of what he did to Callie…but he's never made time for them. Nothing he'd said makes me think that will change. It's sad."

At the nurses' station Diane sat to do paperwork, while Melissa sorted through the vases of old flowers. "How are Josh and Callie adjusting to their new school?"

"Just fine. The teachers are great," Diane said, adding a few notes to a report on a patient who was due to be discharged that afternoon. "I found a house for us to rent in Tipperary Springs. It's walking distance from the school."

"I'm so glad for you!" Melissa said. "Although I'm going to miss having you next door." Her hands full of wilting carnations, she paused suddenly as a thought occurred to her. "Who's going to cook for Gregory and Alice Ann?"

Diane laughed and shook her head. "*You* are. I've shown you how to make every dish I know. And there are a million others in cookbooks and online. If you can read, you can cook."

Melissa threw away the flowers and pulled up another chair. "I promised Gregory to stay on as nanny for three months, and my time is almost up. What should I do?"

Diane set aside the patient's chart. "What do you want?"

"That's just it," she said. "What I want, I can't have. Do I take the crumbs and try to be satisfied? Or do I leave and try to forget?"

Diane took her hands. "If you really love him, you'll never forget."

"I could say nothing and just stay," Melissa said slowly. "I want to care for Alice Ann, but not as a nanny."

"Then tell him how you feel," her friend urged.

Melissa drew back and let out a sigh. "He'll never forgive a woman who's lied to him."

"You might be surprised."

Or she might be hurt. "We'll see."

MELISSA CRANKED UP the volume on her favorite Missy Higgins CD and moved around the cottage kitchen, preparing her dinner. The music was to drown out her thoughts and make her feel less lonely. She'd never minded being on her own before, but now it wasn't simply that she was alone; she was without Gregory.

She heard a knock just as she was about to put her plate of food in the microwave. She left the meal on the counter and went to the door. Opening it, she found herself face-to-face with the man himself.

"I'd like to talk to you," he said. "May I come in?"

Melissa nodded, her heart skipping a beat. He'd never come to the cottage before. What could he want?

He glanced at her plate. "I'm disturbing your dinner. Should I come back later?"

"I was on the phone with Diane." Moaning in her friend's ear about how there was still no word from the nursing school.

"Should I come back later?"

"No." She stepped back, feeling as skittish as a colt. "The food can wait. I was going to have to heat it in the microwave, anyway."

Melissa motioned him into the lounge room. She turned down the volume on the CD player, then sat on the love seat and gestured to one of the two armchairs opposite. A coffee table, a plant stand overflowing with ferns and one of Ally's paintings completed the cozy furnishings.

Gregory sat stiffly, drumming his fingers on his thighs. Melissa watched his sensitive, strong hands. Those hands had touched her breasts....

"What is it?" she demanded, tension making her sound impatient. "Nothing's wrong with Alice Ann, is there?"

"Alice Ann's fine," he said quickly. "Have you spoken to Diane recently? I was able to give her some good news this afternoon."

"I haven't talked to her since yesterday evening when I was moaning that I still haven't heard about my application to nursing school. What's happening? I don't think she'd mind you telling me."

"James is dropping his appeal for custody," Gregory said. "Diane will be sole guardian of Josh and Callie. James has also retracted statements he's made regarding Diane's mental state. He's accepted that the divorce is final. He'll be allowed limited access to his children, but he's promised to have no further contact with Diane."

Melissa breathed out on a whoop of joy. "I can't believe it. That's wonderful!" She jumped to her feet and moved past Gregory to the phone on the breakfast bar. "I'm going to call her right away."

Gregory stood and stopped her with a hand on her arm. "Can you wait just a minute? There's something else."

She searched his face. "What is it?"

"Your three months as nanny are almost up."

"That's right," she said, suddenly wary. Was he going to ask her to leave?

"So, we need to make a decision."

"Whether I go or stay." She finished his thought. "I've been thinking about it."

"And?" he prompted.

"What do *you* want?" she countered, stalling for time.

"I want you to stay."

Something gave way inside her chest. A tension that had lodged there for ages without her being consciously aware of it suddenly dissolved. "In what capacity?" she asked softly.

Instead of answering, he moved closer. She felt the heat from his body and nearly fainted with longing. Tenderly he cradled her face between both hands. A thumb brushed her lip. His breath warmed her cheek. "Like this."

He kissed her.

The ache of love too long suppressed welled to the surface. She wound her arms around his neck and melted into the kiss. Locked in his embrace where she belonged, she gave herself up to the warmth and weight of his hands and his low bass murmur, which vibrated right through to her heart.

And then her uncertainty intruded on the moment. She tried to ignore it, but now that doubt had pierced her mind, nothing could remove it.

"What is it?" Gregory said, pulling back.

"I don't know." Fists clenched at her sides, she paced, annoyed with herself.

She had wanted to do Something Big with her life....

Don't be an idiot, she told herself. Gregory wouldn't stop her from being a nurse. He'd never been anything but supportive of her aspirations. He believed in her. He was certain she'd succeed in whatever she attempted.

But it wasn't *him* that had to believe in her. It was *her.* Until she was accepted into nursing school, she'd never be anything but a volunteer. Anyone could do that. For her own self-esteem she had to accomplish what she'd set out to do. She imagined herself getting rejected. How easy it would be then for her to slip back into Gregory's life. She'd go from being a nanny to a wife and stepmother. But her lost dreams would haunt her. She couldn't bear to go back to being dissatisfied with herself. Gregory didn't need a woman like that in his life. She didn't want to be that person. If she didn't get into nursing school she would have to search for something else. Something that might take her away from Tipperary Springs.

Melissa turned, frowning, because she couldn't believe what she was going to say. "I'm not ready."

His mouth opened, but it was clear he had no idea what to say.

"I don't *know* when I'll be ready."

"Please don't tell me never."

Miserable, she gazed at him. "I'll let you know."

THE LETTER FROM the school of nursing came three days later. Melissa had stopped at the bottom of the driveway to get the mail on her way home from picking up Alice Ann. With the Volkswagen idling, she leafed through the envelopes. Usually, they were mostly bills and the occasional letter for Gregory. Today, her name jumped out at her. The university insignia in the top left-hand corner took her breath away.

She started to tear open the flap, then stopped, her heart pounding. She began to chew on her thumb, then stopped that, too. It was healing nicely, thanks to a short course of antibiotics. Tossing the letters onto the passenger seat, she put the car back into gear. She wouldn't open it with Alice Ann in the car. Melissa wouldn't want the girl to see her cry.

The letter sat on the counter all afternoon while she cleaned the house and played with Alice Ann. Every now and then she'd look at it and be tempted to open it and end the suspense. But as soon as she picked it up, she'd throw it down again. If it was good news, that would be fine. But if she'd been rejected, she would be in limbo once more.

A glance at the clock told her it was time to start dinner. A light rain was falling when she went onto the veranda to call Alice Ann. The girl was riding her bicycle—without the training wheels—and trailing a long stick through the dirt for Wriggles to run after.

In the paddock Ruthie and her litter grazed peacefully. Benny had been moved to Constance's. For the first week Alice Ann had gone over every day to visit. Then one day she'd forgotten. Melissa and Gregory had breathed a sigh of relief.

Nowadays they talked in person for a few minutes every day, catching each other up on news of Alice Ann and the day's events before Melissa went back to the cottage. After that kiss there could be no denying their feelings. But the kiss hadn't been repeated. It wouldn't be until Melissa made up her mind.

"Alice Ann!" she called. "Time to come in."

Melissa went back to the kitchen and assembled the ingredients for the stir-fry she was going to make for dinner. Chicken, vegetables, sauces… She lined them up on the counter, then read the recipe again. It wasn't the first time she'd cooked since Diane had moved away, but it was the first time she'd made something that wasn't prepared in advance. If she made a mistake she couldn't cover it up. But rehearsals were over; it was time to put herself out there.

"Can I help?" Alice Ann's cheeks were rosy with the cold and her hair straggled out of her ponytail.

"Wash your hands and brush your hair," she said. "Then you can trim the snow peas."

The girl ran off to the bathroom. Melissa propped the letter on the windowsill above the sink, next to the African violet, so it wouldn't get food on it. Then she rinsed the peas and put the colander on the table for Alice Ann.

When the girl came back she chattered away about Amy and her other friends at play school. "Next year I'm going to go to a big school," she informed Melissa.

"You're going to do Big Things," Melissa predicted, smiling at her enthusiasm.

"Yes, but I'll still do small things, too," she said comfortably. Patiently, she pulled down the string on a snow pea, just as she'd been shown. Then she beamed up at Melissa, proud of her accomplishment.

Melissa blinked. And did a mental side-step. Suddenly she saw her life, which seemed so confusing and difficult, from a different perspective. Everything clicked into place.

Life was made up of small things. A child's smile. A new skill learned. Shared laughter. All the small things added up to Big Things. Love. Family. Home.

And in the blink of an eye, her perception of the

letter had subtly altered, too. It no longer had a stranglehold over her future. If she didn't get into nursing school this time around, she'd take courses at the technical college and apply again next year. It was so simple she didn't understand why she hadn't seen it before.

Melissa fried the meat first, being careful not to overcook it, then set it aside while she cooked the vegetables. Rice bubbled away in the rice cooker. Finally she threw everything together and added the mixture of sauces, tossing it around to blend the ingredients.

"Alice Ann, can you set the table, please?" she called over her shoulder.

The girl got two plates out of the drawer.

"*Three* places," Melissa corrected. "We'll need three place settings tonight."

"Are you staying for dinner?" Gregory said from the doorway.

Surprised, Melissa put a hand to her heart. "I didn't hear you over the stove fan and the clatter of dishes."

"You're staying for dinner," he repeated, a statement this time, not a query. His gaze met hers, serious and questioning.

Melissa walked over to him and put her arms around his waist. "Actually, I thought I'd stay... forever."

"I'll get another glass," Alice Ann said, and bustled over to the cupboard.

Gregory gathered Melissa closer and held her tightly. "You had me worried."

"*You* were worried—how do you think *I* felt?" She stretched up to kiss him.

Her eyes were closing when he drew back. "What's the news?" he asked, nodding over her shoulder to the letter on the windowsill.

She laughed, a little embarrassed. "I haven't looked."

Gregory let her go and walked over to get it. "Come on."

She refused to take the letter. "*You* open it."

Eyes on her, he slit the envelope open with a knife. Unfolding the single sheet of paper, he scanned it, then glanced up, his expression unreadable.

Melissa's insides churned at the suspense. "Tell me."

Gregory grinned. "You're in."

"I'm in!" Laughing and crying at the same time, she threw her arms around his neck, loving his strength and solidity. Loving *him*.

He picked her up and swung her around. "I knew you'd get there."

"Me, too!" Alice Ann had no idea what they were talking about, but was ready to join in the celebration. Soon they were caught in a three-way embrace.

Melissa felt her joy spill over at the love that filled the warm, homey kitchen. She hadn't known it, but all along she'd been doing Something Big.

* * * * *

Welcome to cowboy country....

Turn the page for a sneak preview of
TEXAS BABY
by
Kathleen O'Brien
An exciting new title from Harlequin
Superromance for everyone
who loves stories about the West.

Harlequin Superromance—
Where life and love weave together in emotional
and unforgettable ways.

CHAPTER ONE

CHASE TRANSFERRED his gaze to the road and iden-
tified a foreign spot on the horizon. A car. Almost
half a mile away, where the straight, tree-lined drive
met the public road. He could tell it was coming too
fast, but judging the speed of a vehicle moving
straight toward you was tricky.

It wasn't until it was about two hundred yards
away that he realized the driver must be drunk...or
crazy. Or both.

The guy was going maybe sixty. On a private
drive, out here in ranch country, where kids or
horses or tractors or stupid chickens might come
darting out any minute, that was criminal. Chase
straightened from his comfortable slouch and
waved his hands.

"Slow down, you fool," he called out. He took
the porch steps quickly and began walking fast
down the driveway.

The car veered oddly, from one lane to another,
then up onto the slight rise of the thick green spring
grass. It just barely missed the fence.

"Slow down, damn it!"

He couldn't see the driver, and he didn't recognize this automobile. It was small and old, and couldn't have cost much, even when it was new. It was probably white, but now it needed either a wash or a new paint job or both.

"Damn it, what's wrong with you?"

At the last minute, he had to jump away, because the idiot behind the wheel clearly wasn't going to turn to avoid a collision. He couldn't believe it. The car kept coming, finally slowing a little, but it was too late.

Still going about thirty miles an hour, it slammed into the large, white-brick pillar that marked the front boundaries of the house. The pillar wasn't going to give an inch, so the car had to. The front end folded up like a paper fan.

It seemed to take forever for the car to settle, as if the trauma happened in slow motion, reverberating from the front to the back of the car in ripples of destruction. The front windshield suddenly seemed to ice over with lethal bits of glassy frost. Then the side windows exploded.

The front driver's door wrenched open, as if the car wanted to expel its contents. Metal buckled hideously. Small pieces, like hubcaps and mirrors, skipped and ricocheted insanely across the oyster-shell driveway.

Finally, everything was still. Into the silence, a plume of steam shot up like a geyser, smelling of rust and heat. Its snakelike hiss almost smothered the low, agonized moan of the driver.

Chase's anger had disappeared. He didn't feel anything but a dull sense of disbelief. Things like this didn't happen in real life. Not in his life. Maybe the sun had actually put him to sleep....

But he was already kneeling beside the car. The driver was a woman. The frosty glass-ice of the windshield was dotted with small flecks of blood. She must have hit it with her head, because just below her hairline a red liquid was seeping out. He touched it. He tried to wipe it away before it reached her eyebrow, though, of course, that made no sense at all. Her eyes were shut.

Was she conscious? Did he dare move her? Her dress was covered in glass, and the metal of the car was sticking out lethally in all the wrong places.

Then he remembered, with an intense relief, that every good medical man in the county was here, just behind the house, drinking his champagne. He found his phone and paged Trent.

The woman moaned again.

Alive, then. Thank God for that.

He saw Trent coming toward him, starting out at a lope, but quickly switching to a full run.

"Get Dr. Marchant," Chase called. "Don't bother with 9-1-1."

Trent didn't take long to assess the situation. A fraction of a second, and he began pulling out his cell phone and running toward the house.

The yelling seemed to have roused the woman. She opened her eyes. They were blue and clouded with pain and confusion.

"Chase," she said.

His breath stalled. His head pulled back. "What?"

Her only answer was another moan, and he wondered if he had imagined the word. He reached around her and put his arm behind her shoulders. She was tiny. Probably petite by nature, but surely way too thin. He could feel her shoulder blades pushing against her skin, as fragile as the wishbone in a turkey.

She seemed to have passed out, so he put his other arm under her knees and lifted her out. He tried to avoid the jagged metal, but her skirt caught on a piece and the tearing sound seemed to wake her again.

"No," she said. "Please."

"I'm just trying to help," he said. "It's going to be all right."

She seemed profoundly distressed. She wriggled in his arms, and she was so weak, like a broken bird. It made him feel too big and brutish. And intrusive. As if touching her this way, his bare hands against the warm skin behind her knees, were somehow a transgression.

He wished he could be more delicate. But he smelled gasoline, and he knew it wasn't safe to leave her here.

Finally he heard the sound of voices, as guests began to run around the side of the house, alerted by Trent. Dr. Marchant was at the front, racing toward them as if he were forty instead of seventy. Susannah was right behind him, her green dress floating around her trim legs.

"Please," the woman in his arms murmured again. She looked at him, the expression in her blue eyes lost and bewildered. He wondered if she might be on drugs. Hitting her head on the windshield might account for this unfocused, glazed look, but it couldn't explain the crazy driving.

"Please, put me down. Susannah... The wedding..."

Chase's arms tightened instinctively, and he froze in his tracks. She whimpered, and he realized he might be hurting her. "Say that again?"

"The wedding. I have to stop it."

* * * * *

Be sure to look for TEXAS BABY,
available September 11, 2007,
as well as other fantastic Superromance titles
available in September.

Welcome to Cowboy Country...

TEXAS BABY

by Kathleen O'Brien

#1441

Chase Clayton doesn't know what to think.
A beautiful stranger has just crashed his
engagement party, demanding that he not
marry because she's pregnant with his baby.
But the kicker is—he's never seen her before.

Look for TEXAS BABY and other fantastic
Superromance titles on sale September 2007.

Available wherever books are sold.

ATHENA FORCE

Heart-pounding romance and thrilling adventure.

Professional negotiator Lindsey Novak is faced with her biggest challenge—to buy back Teal Arnett, a young woman with unique powers. In the process Lindsey uncovers a devastating plot that involves scientists from around the globe, and all of them lead to one woman who is bent on destroying Athena Academy...at any cost.

LOOK FOR

THE GOOD THIEF

by Judith Leon

Available September wherever you buy books.

AF38973

REQUEST YOUR FREE BOOKS!
2 FREE NOVELS PLUS 2 FREE GIFTS!

HARLEQUIN®

Super Romance®

Exciting, emotional, unexpected!

YES! Please send me 2 FREE Harlequin Superromance® novels and my 2 FREE gifts. After receiving them, if I don't wish to receive any more books, I can return the shipping statement marked "cancel." If I don't cancel, I will receive 6 brand-new novels every month and be billed just $4.69 per book in the U.S., or $5.24 per book in Canada, plus 25¢ shipping and handling per book and applicable taxes, if any*. That's a savings of close to 15% off the cover price! I understand that accepting the 2 free books and gifts places me under no obligation to buy anything. I can always return a shipment and cancel at any time. Even if I never buy another book from Harlequin, the two free books and gifts are mine to keep forever.

135 HDN EEX7   336 HDN EEYK

Name	(PLEASE PRINT)
Address	Apt.
City	State/Prov.	Zip/Postal Code

Signature (if under 18, a parent or guardian must sign)

Mail to the **Harlequin Reader Service**®:
IN U.S.A.: P.O. Box 1867, Buffalo, NY 14240-1867
IN CANADA: P.O. Box 609, Fort Erie, Ontario L2A 5X3

Not valid to current Harlequin Superromance subscribers.

Want to try two free books from another line?
Call 1-800-873-8635 or visit www.morefreebooks.com.

* Terms and prices subject to change without notice. NY residents add applicable sales tax. Canadian residents will be charged applicable provincial taxes and GST. This offer is limited to one order per household. All orders subject to approval. Credit or debit balances in a customer's account(s) may be offset by any other outstanding balance owed by or to the customer. Please allow 4 to 6 weeks for delivery.

Your Privacy: Harlequin is committed to protecting your privacy. Our Privacy Policy is available online at www.eHarlequin.com or upon request from the Reader Service. From time to time we make our lists of customers available to reputable firms who may have a product or service of interest to you. If you would prefer we not share your name and address, please check here. ☐

HSR07

The latest novel in The Lakeshore Chronicles
by *New York Times* bestselling author

SUSAN WIGGS

From the award-winning author of *Summer at Willow Lake*
comes an unforgettable story of a woman's emotional journey
from the heartache of the past to hope for the future.

With her daughter grown and flown, Nina Romano is ready to
embark on a new adventure. She's waited a long time for dating,
travel and chasing dreams. But just as she's beginning to enjoy
being on her own, she finds herself falling for Greg Bellamy,
owner of the charming Inn at Willow Lake and a single father
with two kids of her own.

DOCKSIDE

"The perfect summer read." —Debbie Macomber

*Available the first week of August 2007
wherever paperbacks are sold!*

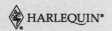

HARLEQUIN®

EVERLASTING LOVE™

Every great love has a story to tell™

Third time's a charm.

Texas summers. Charlie Morrison.
Jasmine Boudreaux has always connected
the two. Her relationship with Charlie
begins and ends in high school. Twenty
years later it begins again—and ends again.
Now fate has stepped in one more time—
will Jazzy and Charlie finally give in to
the love they've shared all this time?

Look for

Summer After Summer

by
Ann DeFee

**Available September
wherever books are sold.**

www.eHarlequin.com

HESAS0907

COMING NEXT MONTH